I0772399

STARSHOT

THE SKYWARD SAGA
BOOK 1

A.R. KNIGHT

I watch her from behind the thick tree as she moves among the ferns and vines, yellowed now from lack of rain. A mosquito buzzes in front of me, but doesn't land thanks to the sticky sap covering my skin, keeping me free to concentrate.

Because she's been getting better.

My mosswrap slides with me as I move around the trunk, its rings of woven, soft green keeping me cool and quiet as I pad out behind her. She, on the other hand, is wearing a stained, ragged shirt, things she calls trousers extend down to her ankles where they meet thick brown—and now hopelessly scratched—boots. They break twigs, snap plants as she moves, making her easy to follow. She wears a shiny gray tube tied to her waist, and I've never seen her use it, but the shiny gray tube is compelling all the same. Today, I'm going to get it.

There's a wild hoot from somewhere ahead—a startled bird, and she whips her eyes towards it, her arms tense, and I make my move. A one-two step over the branch, directly into the clear middle of a pile of fresh-fallen leaves, tapping the silent ground, and then, with a press of my right calf, I jump. I'm too far away for a tackle, but just right for the back of her legs. She manages to catch the moving air and half-turns as I fly into her, which only makes things worse for her balance, as now I'm pushing her sideways rather than forward.

She crumples to the ground with a grunt and I'm on top of her, scrambling for the tube. I get my hand on the hilt when I feel something sharp against my throat.

"Wrong target, Kaishi," Viera whispers. "The knife is deadlier up close than the pistol."

I flick my eyes down to the simple leather hilt and shining metal blade—forged, so Viera says, back in her homeland beneath the mountains. If I ever get my own knife, it'll be black-glass, and it'll shimmer as it sucks in Ignos' light.

"You've never shown me how it works," I say, but I let my hands off her pistol.

Only then does she take the knife away.

"Not going to, either, unless things take a turn." Viera waits for me to get off of her, and then she follows me to her feet, sighing at the new dirt stains on her clothes.

"What kind of turn?"

"A bad one." Viera slots the knife back into the slit near the top of her boot.

Before I can get more details, a mournful call rings through the woods. It's haunting, and it winds through the jungle trees like the spirits of my ancestors. A hollowed caller. One of three we have, and they're all prizes. Blow it from the top of the Tier and you're going to catch its sound even in other villages.

Father says it makes other tribes jealous. Mother says it sings a beautiful song. I don't see why the hollowed caller can't do both.

I'm not waiting for the second blast. I flash a quick thanks at Viera for playing the game and check the vine-tie holding my hair together—there's nothing worse than loose strands catching on branches while sprinting through the forest—and I'm running.

Feet, bare and scuffed, pound dead leaves into dirt as I pad along the pathway back to the main square. Ferns tickle my legs. Trees make half-hearted swipes towards my head.

My route isn't the only way back home, and soon enough I'm seeing motion in the woods around me. Hunters, farmers, people moving because sitting in the village all day is a recipe for losing your mind.

They're all coming back now, and they're not quiet about it. Whoops and calls ring out, greetings mingle with questions and answers about quarry, the weather, and what's cooking. I join in, and nobody cares that the priest's daughter isn't at the ceremony yet.

Because, mostly, I'm the priest's daughter. Not the priest.

Never will be.

When I walk into my village, I see eight stone houses. Built flat, as if someone started out with cubes and then gave up when they realized our stone doesn't play nice with right angles. We don't have etchers, here in the jungle. Our stone comes by our hands. The mortar that binds it together is mixed with the power of our arms, and spread with rocks.

But I'm not looking at the houses. I'm focused on the one thing that keeps our village going. The Tier, and ours is a big one. The largest that I've ever seen, and I've been to some other tribes on tours with my father, seen their Tiers. Rocks dug up from the ground support logs and moss, which we've piled on top of each other to create a living mound. Wherever a slate presents itself, our people have carved their version of Ignos and his burning halo.

Dusk makes for perfect viewing time: Ignos is kissing the far horizon, and plants his last lights right on the Tier's top. On the altar there, a smooth stone slab pinned between twinned pillars bears Ignos' circle wreathed in shards. Anything put on that altar is centered between Ignos, making for an easy transition from this life to the next.

Ignos isn't alone up there now. My father stands in front of the altar with a trio around him. One is holding the hollowed caller—a yellowed stick of bamboo with spaced holes—and I recognize a boy not much older than myself.

Normally he's out hunting with the rest, but apparently he's done something right—you don't get to blow the caller unless you've earned it. The other two are what I call my father's followers. They trail him around town and help him get whatever he needs.

Right now, that's a black-glass knife and a person, pinned with his back on the altar.

"Kaishi!" Mother's voice brings me away from the scene and over towards her. She's standing outside our house with a look that promises a thousand punishments if I don't veer her way this second, so I do.

"I'm not late," I say the words to kill the fight before it starts. I fail, and I know this by the measure of my mother's right eyebrow and how high it rises.

"Don't presume to know what I'm about to say," Mother scolds. "It's rude, and childish."

"Aren't children supposed to be childish?" I say, because I've so far escaped the rite of adulthood: getting a husband or a wife.

Don't get me wrong—I'm a fan of this. Plenty of nice, unattached hunters in our village, but there's a resistance I have to destiny. Or rather, what others think is my destiny. But I keep quiet about that because I'm not suicidal.

"Clearly," Mother replies. I think Father loves her, in part, because she has this razor sarcasm and she's not afraid to cut with it. "It's not what you have done, but what you haven't."

Now she points me back towards the Tier and I can trace that finger with the sense of a child being told just where their mistake lies. It's the black-glass knife, the one now held by Father. He's raising it high to catch the Ignos' light, so that it practically glows up there.

And I know.

"I forgot," I say, which is the truth.

Honest.

"Yes. Your father cleaned it himself."

"We don't usually have sacrifices every day."

"This isn't a usual time," but before Mother can continue the lecture, the hollowed caller blows again.

This time it's a staccato blast. If you're not here now, it's saying, you're going to miss something good, so Mother closes her mouth into a tight frown, grabs my arm like I've seen six summers instead of sixteen, and we're off.

My tribe isn't small, but we compress well into tight rows for the ceremony. There's an aisle in the middle, where, in a few minutes, the body currently on the altar will be carried. My mother pulls me right between the gathered people. We're all wearing our moss-wraps; emerald and brown mosses that we grow and weave together. Some tribes have fur, others use cotton, but we're too deep beneath the trees for that.

Any parts the moss doesn't cover, and plenty that it does, we coat with various salves; stuff that helps keep the bugs away or helps heal cuts and bites. The smells mingle with burning incense, another village feature and the core of one of my favorite things: taking a sprint along the outskirts of the town and enjoying the scents. Right now it's a spicy smoke, and at the edges I inhale the first hints of dinner: Pork, buried earlier in the day with hot coals.

I'm not the only one thinking about food; we pass by a young boy, half my age or less, who, because he's surrounded by his towering parents and other adults, can't see what's going on and is taking the loss of opportunity to stare back towards the cook fires. I seize a moment and tap him on the shoulder.

Come with me, I mouth. The time for talking is past—Father has already started the prayers—but the boy gets it. Takes my offered hand and heads with us to the front of the crowd. The perks of being the priest's daughter? A front row spot for every sacrifice.

Blood spatters come free.

You might think the offer on the altar would struggle. He's likely a hunter, though I don't recognize the tattoos on this one. He's probably been taught to fight, to kill and take what he can to survive. Only here he's being held by an older man covered in feathered bracelets, whose arm is bony and, while strong, is no more capable of keeping a man like our sacrifice down than I would be.

Only the captive lies still.

Honor.

That's what Father tells me the first time I witness one of these. The sacrifice honors Ignos and brings some glory to our tribe, but it's also redemption for our captive. A chance for him to reclaim some of what he's lost by getting captured in the first place.

Go to Ignos in peace and accept your place in his home, and be glad of it.

The argument doesn't work with every sacrifice, though. Some fight to the end. Struggle and plead. Those are always the messy ones. I try to look away when those happen, but Mother forces me to watch. To witness the disgrace.

Fighting when there's no chance makes it all hurt more.

Father goes through another set of prayers. He's asking Ignos for water, for food, and for a healthy tribe. It's the standard trio, and I don't fault him for lacking originality. Neither does the rest of the village, and we all say our parts when we should.

The next part is rough, but the captive makes it easy. Several quick cuts with the black glass blade and we're looking at his heart. Father's holding it up to Ignos' last light as it touches the head of the carved altar.

Then it's done. No lightning, thunder, or earthquakes. If Ignos heard, he's not making it obvious.

When the crowd goes, the boy squirms away with them, leaving me alone with Mother. She doesn't want to get started again with everyone here, and I'm thinking it's partly because nobody has an appetite for fighting after watching someone get ripped apart, literally, right in front of them. So we stand and wait, because my one job is coming down the steps towards me.

Father, softening the gesture with a broad smile, hands me the blood-soaked black glass knife with both hands. I accept it in the same way, and the warm liquid slips between my fingers. I try not to think that the red was, moments ago, inside someone and only succeed when Father starts talking to me.

"You'll have it cleaned this time, Kaishi?" he says the words without malice, with the hint of a joke, because Father knows I've already heard it from Mother. "We have been lucky. There's another one ready for tomorrow."

"Do you think he heard it?" I ask. "Ignos?"

"It's not whether he heard our prayers," Father replies. "But whether we deserve an answer."

He is described in superlatives. A living weapon. Death incarnate. The last thing you see before your eyes go dark. All of these and more, on a hundred worlds, have been used to whisper about his coming.

More generally, and to himself, he goes by the name he has earned:

Sax.

A single syllable, because he is as of yet a three-letter Oratus. No ship under his command, no army at his beck and call. Not that he needs or wants those; each would take him away from the blood. From the visceral feel of his claws doing the work they're made for.

He's looking at them now. Checking them in front of a broad mirror. All twenty of them. Five on each hand, and he has four of those. They're attached to arms: two on each side, sprouting from a long torso that, due to his gray scales, shimmers like rippling water on a cloudy day. Twin legs, a tail and his head, thick and dominated by his large oval eyes and wrap-around mouth, round out the limbs. Nearly four meters tall, Sax doesn't come in a small package.

As he checks his body's weapons, Sax keeps an eye on the Oratus next to him. Same body, same height, only Bas is closer to rose gold in color. Sax looks at her with a mix of confidence and love, the sort of bond shared by a Pair.

Bas doesn't notice, because she's already started putting on her mask. She presses her left foreclaw—the upper set of arms—into the mirror. At first, it seems like the claw might push through and shatter the thing. Send glass everywhere. Instead, the surface of the glass warps; sucks in her claw and then oozes out over it. Liquid metal.

The mask flows forward over Bas's claw, her arm and the rest of her. Once Bas is completely covered, eyes and all, the mask appears to sink into her skin. Becomes translucent, as though her pinkish scales were covered by a slight fog.

Sax follows her lead. They all need masks; required for missions with a high risk of attack or exposure to vacuum, and this one has both. Behind him, he hears, or rather, through cavities in his skull full of tiny, vibration-sensing antennae, detects the other half of their set laughing. The usual for those two. Go back to the beginning of their fifty mission stretch and you'd find Sax seething at their hissing.

Now, he ignores it.

When the time comes, Gar and Lan won't be laughing. They'll pull the triggers on their miners, same as Sax. Gar would probably shoot first.

The mask is cool, but quickly warms to Sax's skin. It actually burns a little. Increases Sax's body temperature to ideal levels for performance. While the mask is getting to equilibrium, Sax and Bas step back from the mirror to see the next part of the show.

Oratus claws are like diamonds—they can cut through just about anything—but they're not much help against an enemy at range. The mask helps against weapons fire, but pop enough holes in it, and the mask will fall apart too. Better to eliminate the problem.

The mirror helps them with that. With a wave of Sax's claw, the mirror flows up towards the ceiling and reveals blue metal shelves holding an array of deadly tools. Sax moves first, with the confidence of knowing exactly what he wants and how to get it. The target is a pair of black sticks about my height.

Sax calls them batons. He picks them up with his foreclaws and sets them across his back. They stick to the mask, like a magnet.

Next comes a belt for his waist, followed by a variety of fun and games. Things to be thrown, fired, or tasted, depending on the situation. Next to him, Bas makes her own choices, and when they're both done, they take a second to stare at each other. Check the list, make sure nobody's forgotten something.

Neither of them has.

"Evva says this might be the last one," Bas breaks the silence, and while her mouth moves, the sound actually comes through the mask.

The four of them are already connected.

"There are always more," Sax replies, his voice like grinding sand.

"But what if it is?"

"Then we'll have to find something else to kill," Gar joins the conversation, and their group, in the center of the room. There's not much to say to that, because everyone agrees with Gar's assessment. Oratus are like miners—they serve a purpose, and Sax has a hard time thinking of what that might be if not to tear the galaxy's enemies apart. Lan saves him the trouble by joining in, completing their set.

They're ready to go.

3 / NIGHT RITUALS

I'm holding the torch in both hands and watching the flames dance to the nighttime breeze. It's not heavy—the stick of wood isn't much longer than my forearm, and the burning rag doesn't send the fire high—but Father says that holding with two hands signals devotion to the task.

As I'm going to offer a prayer to Ignos, the god that determines whether my family and tribe lives or dies, devotion seems appropriate.

It's dark in the jungle after Ignos goes down. If I'm standing in the village, where most of the trees have been cut to make room, I could see the stars. Underneath the canopy, though, I'd be wading in a sea of black without the torch. As it is, my eyes can't make out much more than my own feet and the overgrown path beneath them.

My ears, though, find a world of their own.

While bird calls drop away as Nomis—the silver sister of Ignos—rises, other animals take their place. Buzzing insects swarm around the light, some of them as large as my hand. The sap I've spread over my skin keeps most off of me, and years of practice mean I don't flinch when a moth lands on my wrist and flares its owl-eyed wings.

My steps startle a spider monkey somewhere above, and it hoots as it swings away, alerting its family to my coming.

Fear doesn't strike me here, even though I'm alone. Our hunters, and those of other tribes, cross these areas enough that any large predators have either learned to stay away or found themselves in our fires. Those same tribes don't have an interest in taking me, even if they were out at night. Sacrifices are about honoring Ignos, and a sixteen year-old girl doesn't have much honor to provide.

Not yet, anyway.

When I reach the clearing, there's a small stone totem standing at the far end. About as tall as I am, and bearing another carving of Ignos. This one, though, is white-spotted and washed out. Father says it's been here since before the village, and that it's partly the reason why our tribe has survived so long; others make pilgrimages here for their own people, and their gifts pay their peaceful passage. Food and tools that help our village grow.

I'm the only one here now, though, which is good. Solitude helps me get closer to Ignos, or at least that's what I think as I kneel before the totem and begin the rites. With my eyes closed, I set the torch to the side, though I have to twist it into the hard dirt. A sign we could use some rain—normally this clearing is a muddy mess. Everyone knows when you've been here because you come back with coated knees.

It's a ritual prayer. Asking for guidance, strength, and the usual array of graces. Only at the end do I break into originality. Start a one-sided conversation with a god that is so great and mystifying that I have no idea if he can understand me, or if he cares.

"I don't know if you're listening," I say, and I put my hands on the totem. We're not supposed to touch it, but nobody's watching, and maybe it'll get Ignos' attention. "I'm asking you for something tonight. Again."

I pause. This is the hard part, because when I don't say it then it doesn't feel so real. I can distract away the feeling with my chores, or conversation, or just by running through the jungle. But I didn't come here to be distracted, so I say it anyway.

"I need a destiny. Father says I can't be a priest, and Mother tells me I'll be getting a husband soon. I don't want that, Ignos. I don't want what they want for me. Show me something else, please!"

It's a plea, and I'm a little ashamed as I say it. Blushing, even, there in the dark, because I know most of the village would say the same thing if they had the chance, but they don't. They make do with the struggles, and embrace the happy moments: a successful harvest, a dance around the fires, a hunt that brings back enough to feed the family.

Who am I to ask for more?

I'm opening my mouth to take it all back, beg forgiveness, when a breeze kicks up and I feel my torch go out. My eyes open to the purest dark I've seen in a while, though I'm able to pick up the torch by the heat of it. Not the first time this has happened, and every Solare knows how to pick their way through the ferns and trees at night.

The dark, though, is why, when the whole sky burns a minute later, I go blind.

Only for a second, and it's not really blindness but shock at the white burst overwhelming everything. I blink rapidly as the glow recedes to a single, huge ball hurtling above the trees. The leafy canopy means I catch the fire in spots as it barrels close and then over my head.

It's hard to see anything in that angry orange and black, but I track the burning ball anyway. At least until it vanishes beneath the tree tops. First comes the snapping and cracking of trees, and then a rippling bang. Like a thunderstorm letting loose over a lake. The ground shifts and I fall to all fours, my fingers digging into the dirt like it's a cliff I'm trying to climb.

Then it's done.

· · ·

Stillness takes over and for a moment everything is stunned quiet. I take a breath. The first insects test their buzzing. Gradually, the jungle restarts its symphony.

When I stand, holding the burned-out torch, I don't turn back towards my village. I saw where the bright flash landed. It didn't look far. I'm thinking of my prayer, too. And destiny.

Ignos might have heard me, and given me an answer. All my parent's stories about heroes started with one thing: when given the chance, the hero acted. So I move past the totem, take a walk into the uncut brush.

It's slow going without a light and wandering into unfamiliar territory. Bugs bite—ants and other critters undeterred by my sap coating—and animals running away from the crash find me and turn around.

Unseen branches scratch my face and a thorn leaves its mark on my hand. I don't turn back, though, because I know what lies behind me.

Eventually I break through into what wasn't a clearing moments before. Now it's a fiery disaster. Trees hold bits of flame like I might hold a cup of water. Dirt and rocks are piled up everywhere, as though someone went digging with abandon. I notice too that most of the debris are black, and hot.

I step onto the dirt.

It sears the soles of my feet, so I dance until I find a bit of slightly cooler rock, then take a look.

There's a pit in the middle, almost as large as one of our houses. Deeper than I am tall, and in the center is something that, to me, appears like an oval boulder. In the flickering orange, it's obviously pitted too. Bits and pieces taken out of its sides, though the unmarked parts shine. I've never seen anything like it, but that meshes with what I'm thinking. Ignos' sent along something completely new.

Something just for me.

I take the next steps slow and careful. Test the dirt to make sure each step isn't too hot. Even so, burns get added to my growing list of injuries.

Never let it be said that Ignos doesn't make you work for your dreams.

I clamber to the edge of the hole. Now that I'm closer, I can tell the oval isn't too much larger than Father. Four or five of him, squashed into the same shape, would make for the entire thing.

As though the oval knows I'm looking at it, it begins to steam. White streams emerge from what grows to be a line around the middle of the oval, floating up into the sky. Then, before I can decide what to do, the oval pops in half. The top part rises up and falls away from me and I notice it's attached with a small silver hinge to the oval's far side.

What's more interesting, though, is what's inside Ignos' gift. It looks like a black sea, though when I concentrate, I can pick out traces of purple. The ink—because I don't know what else to call it—appears still, and I take that as a sign to come closer.

I'm not completely convinced; I take the descent into the pit slow and make sure to identify the easiest way to scramble out if the oval turns out to be unfriendly.

I reach out with one hand to touch the oval's outer shell. The lip of the opening. It's warm, though not as hot as parts of the dirt. If my mind wasn't in total shock, I might wonder why, but instead I note that it's safe to touch and keep going closer.

Both of my hands are on the lip, which rises just about to my chin, and I'm peering into that purple-black ink. There's something in there. I can make out a shadow, shifting in the firelight.

I reach for it, trained by years of grabbing at fish, slip on that narrow lip, and fall inside.

4 / THE ORDER

Sax raises a single claw and the ship takes note. The mirrors slide back into place and hide the remaining weapons. Behind Sax, a door, till that moment unified with the pearly sheen of the ship's walls, shunts open with the hiss of compressed air. Careful not to let his tail get in the way, Sax leads the group from the room and down the ship's outer corridor.

And stops immediately. He's forgotten what Evva said. They're late to the fight, and as the ship's outer hull turns translucent—a neat effect of well-placed screens—the four of them bear witness to chaos.

What look like whole flocks of birds dip and dart through space. A black palette marred by the orange gas giant staring at them, its churning atmosphere dotted with specks as ships criss-cross in front of it. Constant light shows erupt as pilots try their hands with energy weapons, though Sax knows there are plenty more projectiles flying through that vacuum; invisible and just as deadly.

Sax is drawn to the biggest blot of the bunch. Makes sense—that's what he's here for. It's a disc, sort of, and it hangs there in space, dwarfing everything around it. You'd think it would be the center of the fight, seeing as it's the most important ship here, but it looks like the battle has drawn away from it.

"They've set us up," Sax says. "Should be a smooth ride."

"How many do you think, on a seed ship that size?" Gar asks the question, and Sax can almost hear him salivating.

"Enough for all of us, and more besides," Sax replies. "Evva says you'll have to share, Gar."

The commander said nothing of the kind, but that's the implication Sax had when Evva told him they were going with a full assault crew. At least four shuttles, stocked to the brim with soldiers. Sax had made sure they were the only Oratus though. Nobody to take his credit. Still, this is a big commitment for the Chorus military, the Vincere.

"So long as they understand they're getting the scraps and no more," Gar hisses.

At the end of the hall, a circular door spins open. Evva's on the other side. Not directly, but standing in a Sphere. From their eyes, it looks like she's stuck her head into a giant, bluish ball. On the inside, Evva is seeing everything the sensors can give her about the fight and letting her float around in it like some sort of god. Sax has tried it before. It twisted his stomach around and cost him a good meal.

Beyond Evva is the rest of the bridge. Aside from the seemingly huge windshield—screens again, overlaid on heavy armor—the bridge is consumed by pods. Flaum, furry creatures with big eyes and long snouts, sit at some, chattering to each other or to ships outside. Sax resists the urge, though Lan's low growl says she doesn't.

Normally, these things are prey. Normally, they're snacks to tear apart on course to the real meat.

Evva leaves the Sphere before Sax gets through his hypothetical destruction of the Flaum, and she's everything Sax would expect a fourth letter Oratus to be. Her lime green scales are scatter-shot with luminous medals, as though someone had blasted Evva with a cannon full of honors. Each one glows in the light, playing rainbow tricks on Sax's eyes.

"We are ready to begin, commander," Sax says, though a flash behind Evva—some ship meeting a fiery end—draws his eyes away from her.

"Your shuttle is ready," Evva replies. Her voice, not through the masks, sounds filtered until Sax looks back at her. Then the mask reshuffles priorities and brings Evva's next sentence in clear and clean. "Your orders are to proceed directly to the core. Find the Seed Sevora and eliminate it. No need for prisoners."

"Of course," Sax replies.

"You should all know," Evva says, and Sax perks up because her voice has changed. It's not the commander talking, it's Evva. "The Chorus declared a tenth cycle. The Great Peace, they're calling it. It's up to us to deliver that here, make it so the last nine cycles of war aren't wasted."

"The Great Peace? We're still fighting," Bas says.

"Not for much longer," Evva motions a claw out towards space.

"We think this is their last one. The final seed ship. Destroy it, and we've finally won."

Evva's injecting emotion there, and Sax knows why. She's alone on this bridge for a reason. Brilliance, sure, but also because her pair vanished in a seed ship raid gone wrong. Oratus keep their grudges deep, and Evva's gives the four of them a boost.

"We honor your lives," Evva continues, back in formal form.

"We are honored to serve," Sax replies, and hears the others say the same.

It's going to be a good hunt.

5 / MEETING A GOD

When I wake up I know I'm suffocating. I can feel, pressing against my eyes, the cool liquid that must be the ink inside the oval. I also feel my nerves tell me someone's staring my way.

I'm not alone.

As I move my arms—the ink is sludge-like, heavier than I expected—something twitches in my brain. Like a headache blinking on and off, only sharper. I push past it because what I need right now is air.

My feet hit the oval's hard bottom and press, raising my head clear. The ink doesn't drip away clean. It sticks, like fruit juice. I start brushing it away from my mouth, gulp in the first gasp of air, and that's when noises erupt in my head. A mix of animal cries, grinding rock, and sounds that I can't identify at all. They cluster together, writhe and burst, and dimly, beyond, I can still make out the crackle of dying flames and nothing else around the oval.

That, more than anything, confirms that I'm only hearing this in my own head. That, more than anything, drives a stake of fear into my heart.

Fear.

The word appears. Like a dream, or a sudden inspiration. Along with it comes a crystal clear tone, as if the word were spoken by, say, a blown hollowed caller. Not the right sound at all.

Fear.

The word comes again, along with the tone, but this time there's adjustments, like speech, as it climbs through the letters. Like a child learning to sound out a word. Like I did when I was young.

I look down at the ink I'm swimming in, and I find that it's lower than I thought. No, it's evaporating. Vanishing into the night. The pool shrinks until it's barely up to my waist.

I.

Yes, I think, that's me.

Me.

I shake my head. Try knocking it from side to side to see if something might pop out. Or if I've broken part of my brain and it's causing these strange bursts. The motion only makes my ears ring.

New words take time.

It's a sentence and not something I just said. I freeze. Maybe, I think, if I stop doing anything else I'll be able to tell what's going on. Really, I'm reaching for anything. Running through what my tribe teaches when a predator's encountered.

Or an enemy.

Not an enemy.

It's responding to me. The tones are saying the words as they flash into my mind, though I'm not hearing them in my ears, exactly. More like when I imagine someone speaking to me and I can hear their voice despite them not actually talking. It's a feeling.

I'm not your imagination.

That much is obvious. Even though I'm a dreamer, I'm not this good at fooling myself. So I launch to the next question: if this isn't my imagination, and it isn't outside of me, then what is it?

You are Kaishi?

How does it know my name?

I know much more than that, Kaishi. I know where you were born.

I know your father is the priest of your village. And I know you hate cutting your hair.

My name and Father's position, I could excuse. Common enough knowledge for people that live around here. Even neighboring tribes know who my father is, and I've been to a few of them on trading trips, so I could be recognized, though the lack of light in this pit would make it difficult.

But my hair? I've never told a soul.

I never complain, even when Mother takes the knife to my tangled knots. It's a chance to be brave, after all.

Getting through that logic brings me back to my question.

Namely, what is this?

The voice doesn't respond. Then my left arm goes numb. I look at it, start to move my right to touch it, when that goes numb too. My legs twinge, and suddenly I can't feel anything.

Interesting. There seems to be a problem with you, Kaishi.

I agree with that. To add to things, there are sounds coming from the jungle now. Whistles and shouts. I recognize the voices and calls. My own tribe, probably coming to see what happened over here.

Meanwhile, I'm stuck in the oval, unable to feel my toes.

Yes, that is a side effect. The issue appears to be with total control. That I cannot achieve it.

Total control of what?

You.

There is one thing I know of that can control a person if it wishes to. One thing with the power to make a Solare act different than normal, and that is Ignos.

The idea connects the fragments for me. Pulls together the prayer at the totem, the strange flash in the sky and now the voice in my mind. This voice, this thing talking to me, must be Ignos, or at least a part of him.

I wait for the voice to confirm, but it's silent. I'm, however, happy to keep running down this thought. If Ignos is talking to me, why? Couldn't he do as he wished without messing with my head?

Even a god needs to see the world through his subject's eyes.

The sounds are getting louder and I'm guessing Father's warriors will be breaking into the clearing any second. I'd love to get out of the oval, but I still can't move my arms and legs.

First, look down.

I follow Ignos' instructions and glance at the bottom of the oval. The ink is almost all gone, and in the last bit there is a strange green cube. It's a brighter green than any I've seen before—the closest being a newly sprouted leaf on a spring morning. It's crawling with spidery blue veins.

Take it.

As Ignos says the words, my arms are free to move again. Legs too. I'm tempted to run, but angering the god inside my head seems like a poor choice, so I reach and put the palm of my hand on the cube. It jitters slightly, like a scared animal. Then the veins snap off the green cube and reach back towards my hand. I try to jerk away, but the veins have me.

Stay still. It will hurt less.

Now Ignos tells me, after the veins have their tiny hooks in my skin. They're wrapping themselves around my hand, and crawling up to my wrist. I manage to quell my nerves, partly because I'm so covered with cuts and bites already that a few more barely register.

The cube melts and I watch as what was once solid breaks apart and flows up along the blue veins. Over my hand—it's like sap, only not sticky—and around my wrist. The green streams coil around me and, suddenly, harden. Like a torch going out, the green fades to a grim brown.

I call it the Cache. We'll need it.

Ignos' voice sounds pleasant as he says this. Like he's describing a flower, or breakfast. I don't have time to ask why, though, as I see the ferns around the pit split open to reveal the mighty warriors of Father's tribe. They're carrying spears, slings, bows, and they're all staring at me in confusion.

Which, I would be too if I were them.

There's not a story, a lesson from Mother, or an ancient saying that describes what to do if a god takes up residence in your head. So my wide eyes match the tribe's and I answer their silent questions with the only thing I can think of, "I found something."

This doesn't help anyone, but it does spur Father to break through the line of warriors and scramble down into the pit. He rushes over the dirt and, reaching into the oval, pulls me out. I'm not a baby, though, so I have to help him. Use my own legs to climb over the lip. I'm overjoyed that they both work, that the numbness is gone, and in that instant happiness I start to talk because now I'm not staring at a crowd, I'm looking at my father's concerned face.

"It's a gift, Father," I say. "Ignos answered my prayer. He's with me now."

Father takes this the same way I would have if one of the villagers had told me the master of all creation had taken up residence in their mind. He tilts his head, closes his eyes briefly, and then looks past me to the oval. Notices that it's empty.

"A gift," Father speaks slowly, like he did when I was little and he wanted me to stop crying.

I'm annoyed that he doesn't immediately understand, so I repeat the words, "He came from the sky, Father. Ignos is talking to me right now."

That last bit is a stretch. Ignos isn't talking now, and I don't know why. Later, I'll understand that his frequent silences are when he's processing new information. Taking in all the things he doesn't know and understand, and then comparing them to the Cache, the bracelet on my wrist, to see if there's something similar inside its stores.

"Ignos speaks to you?" Father says. He doesn't drop the skeptical tone. "What is he saying?"

Say what I tell you. As if I were speaking it.

Ignos' command comes charging through my mind, and strings of words follow it. Fantastical descriptions of stars and worlds far beyond our own. It doesn't make sense, but I've been raised to trust what a god tells me, so I repeat it anyway. As I talk, Father's expression does work, twisting between confusion, disbelief, and fear.

"All of these things, unknown to you and your tribes, are part of my kingdom," I say as Ignos directs. "It is now time to prepare for you to join that kingdom, which is why I am here. Call your neighboring tribes and bring them to heed my words so that we can begin."

Ignos goes on, through me, about miracles to come. The words are grand and sweeping. The sort of speech Father might make, but that I have never done. This, I think, convinces Father more than anything. Wondrous stories I can make up. Sermons like this take more effort. Require knowing the emotional cadence of the crowd.

Ignos does. I do not.

At the end of Ignos' speech, Father steps back from me. I see a new look in his eyes, one that brings with it a twist of knotted pain. I'm not his daughter in that look. I'm something else. Both feared and revered. I turn away from that hurting stare and see the warriors have been listening, and it's even worse with them: Some are on their knees, bowing towards me. Others are openly weeping or looking up at the sky in search of the miracles I promised.

Father interrupts with a call to go back to the village. A pair of warriors stay behind to look over the oval and search for anything I might have missed. The rest escort us back.

The village is wide awake waiting for us, and our crew breaks apart into a dozen re-tellings of my words. Father takes no time for any of them, instead pulling me to our family's house. As Father leads me inside, he looks at Mother and says, "Our daughter claims she has been touched by Ignos."

Then he turns to me, and with as grave an expression as I've ever seen, says, "She will need to sleep, as tomorrow will bring her first ceremony. If Kaishi speaks the rites well, then our village will have a new priestess. If she does not, then Ignos will not brook her mockery, and we will have another sacrifice."

6 / FLYING IN

They're already hanging as the rest of the grunts enter the shuttle. Flaum, their furry bodies coated in standard-issue hardplate uniforms and Whelks, who wear nothing and carry their rifles in their ocher, stubbly gel arms. Both species birthed in prolific numbers, which is why they fill the vast majority of the sub-roles necessary to keep the Vincere up and running.

Gar, if Sax asks him, would rate the Flaum higher than the slug-like Whelks, but only because Gar prefers the taste of fur.

Sax has his four arms and two legs wrapped around the bars on the roof inside of their assault shuttle. Bas is next to him, and Gar and Lan have similar poses on other bars behind. It's a ridiculous look to the soldiers below, but they know not to point and laugh because the ones who do tend to meet swift, terrible ends.

Besides, there's a point to the exercise. One that Sax knows is coming now that the shuttle has lurched into motion. They're leaving the command ship and starting the cruise through battle-filled space.

If Evva's done her job, then the rest of the Vincere fleet will be running cover for them. Their fighters and frigates ought to be filling every possible attack route with more firepower than even the Sevora care to brave.

The front of the shuttle—on these, the pilots stay at the back—shifts translucent. Ahead of them, growing steadily larger, sits the orange gas giant and the seed ship. A perfect view of their target.

"How many fall in the first minute?" Bas asks the four of them, through the masks. "Half?"

She's talking about their soldiers, below. Sax doesn't need to hear the creatures to know they're nervous, as fodder ought to be before it runs into death.

"A third," Lan replies. "It's a seed ship, not a war vessel. They won't be ready."

"We've given them enough notice," Sax says and the other three hiss in agreement. Leaping late to a fight is bad enough, but it's taken them too long to get the shuttles loaded and ready to launch. Which means Vincere command didn't think a seed ship would be here, this far outside of populated space.

As they get closer, Sax picks out the quadrant divides that slice up the seed ship. Four sections with a circle in the middle. That's where the Seed Sevora would be. The one running the whole operation. Get to that creature and Sax could set the ship on a death spiral into the gas giant. Let the planet's gravity do the rest.

The seed ship's outer hull appears a faded green, which confirms Lan's assessment. The emerald color means the Sevora want this one to start new worlds. Get new species. A red seed ship would be militarized and ready to deliver thousands of battle-ready troops to a target.

Vincere logs say there used to be plenty of other colors too, but Sax hasn't seen those. He briefly wonders why the Sevora would color-code their ships and asks the group, but they don't have an answer and he lets the question drop.

Besides, it's prep time.

"Stim up," Sax says, and everyone, except Bas, who claims she doesn't like the stuff, dips one of their foreclaws into a small vial of bluish liquid held on their belts.

The Stim sticks to his claw as he brings it out of the vial, which has a membrane that seals itself after he's dipped, and Sax raises the coated claw to his mouth. Opens slightly and sticks the claw inside. Licks, with his forked tongue, the Stim off.

Tastes like sugar.

Stim hits him hard. It always does. But it's the sort of slam that's fun. Sax's dual hearts spool up to hyper speed, his pupils blow wide, and there's a slowing that happens. Like someone's told the universe to take a breath. Sax has time to contemplate the shuttle, to check his miners, his mask, and confirm the others in the set are doing the same.

Time too to look up.

To see their shuttle ram into the seed ship's hard metal hull.

7 / CEREMONY

A trio of hunters move a boar, freshly dressed and cleaned, into a pit full of hot coals warmed in one of the many cooking fires. They waste no time shoveling more coals and dirt over the top. It'll cook over the course of the ceremony and be ready to serve as the celebratory dinner.

I'm watching all this as I hack at a coconut under the tilting light of Ignos. The sweet milk inside is going to be cool even on a hot, sweaty afternoon like this one. It's been almost a full day with a god in my head, and Ignos, it turns out, likes to talk. Though I'm guessing the coconut fascinates him, because he stays quiet until I chop a small hole. When I lift the coconut up and taste the first bit of cool, sugary milk, though, Ignos breaks through into my head so fast that I almost spit up everywhere.

Fascinating! I would say that the berries on Vimelia are quite a bit more succulent, however, and not quite as sweet.

He's been using words like those too. Things I don't understand. At first I asked questions, but when those led to equally strange answers, I gave up. I figure Ignos has a lot going on that humans aren't meant to understand anyway.

Also, I have a ceremony to worry about.

Fear not, Kaishi. Everything I'm telling you will make sense eventually.

I'm not worried about Ignos' nonsense. I'm concerned about how I'm supposed to preach to hundreds of my own tribe. Father's words last night weren't idle ones either; it's not unheard of among the tribes to have someone claim they're hearing from Ignos directly. It usually follows that they're proved wrong when one of their "miracles" goes awry. The punishment for that sort of thing is a swift trip to the top of the Tier.

They don't come back down. Not in one piece, anyway.

So now I'm planning my phrases. Running them through as I sip from the coconut.

Do you not trust me, Kaishi? I will give you the words, as I did last night.

Words like those would get me killed. Ignos surprised everyone, sure, but those were ramblings in the middle of midnight to a group of tired warriors seeing something they'd never seen before. None of what Ignos said came from our sacred rites, and promises of far away stars wouldn't do anything for families hoping for rain right here in the jungle.

Father always says that being a priest is about delivering hope and softening despair, so I'm trying to figure out how to do that.

I've seen many speeches delivered, Kaishi. In places far beyond your imagining. In words beyond your comprehension. Trust that I can find the right thing to say.

I look up at the trees framing our village, at the Tier standing tall. On many of those trees, small ants scurry back and forth in search of food. Owls and spider monkeys hang on branches, engaging in their own daily rituals. Bird calls ring through the air; mates exchanging news. If Ignos could understand all of them, then perhaps he could give me the words I needed.

Look at your wrist, Kaishi. That's where we'll find what we want.

The bracelet is still there, tight. I tried to take it off last night, but it wouldn't budge, so I gave up. Too tired then to care much. As I look at it, the dull brown seems to flash green for a moment, as if it knows, somehow.

Every recorded speech we have lives in the Cache. I'll find the right one, and your people will hold you up as the greatest priestess in Solare history.

Did I mention that Ignos has a penchant for hyperbole? He might be a god, but the rate he speaks about me becoming a legend of this and a queen of that is a little much, even for my ambition-starved soul. Part of me is even insulted—does Ignos really think we're this easy to fool?

I'm not trying to trick you, Kaishi. Once we have their hearts, we can use the Cache to find the miracles to capture their minds. Then, you'll have everything you could ever dream of.

I shake my head, which causes my father, who's walking my way, to quirk a smile at me. It's a different version of his usual grin. One that's sad in the corners.

"Deep in conversation with Ignos?" Father says as he takes a seat next to me.

"You could say that," I reply. "Have you ever spoken with him?"

Father shakes his head. "I pray to him, and his replies come in wordless forms. From what I see with you, however, I think I prefer it that way."

I laugh, and it threatens to veer into a sob. Ignos' descent towards the horizon is bringing what's about to happen into focus and the idea that this may be the last time Father and I are going to sit here talking shrivels me up inside. Father, in that way parents do, senses this and puts a hand on my shoulder. The pressure helps. It's a base for me to stand on.

"You know the rites," Father says. "You've heard me speak them often enough. Say the simple ones and you'll be accepted."

Yes, I know them. Prayers for rain, for food, for health. They're not difficult.

They won't make you a legend either.

"You really think those will be good enough?" I ask. "How many are coming?"

"I don't know. We sent runners, but it seems our neighbors are nervous. Last night's event hasn't helped. Nor have they."

I see where he's nodding, and I know what he's talking about because how could I not? Viera's been staying in the guest house for nearly two months now, after her friends left. She's pale-skinned, and she's a Lunare, so she's either here to kill us or trade with us.

I don't tell him about the games we play, what Viera's been teaching me. Some things Father doesn't need to know.

"She's the only one left," I offer.

"For now," Father replies. "Viera makes no secret that her friends are coming back."

"I thought they were good for us. They traded with all the tribes?"

"With one eye on everything we would not give them, like your mother's necklace and my headdress." Father is really talking about the turquoise. Those bright blue gems belong with the priest and his wife, whomever that is.

I don't have anything to say to that and Father sighs a moment later, stands and holds out his hand for me to take. I do and he pulls me up. Places his palms on my shoulders and draws me in for a hug.

"Kaishi, convince them you hear what the Ignos' says," Father whispers. "Our village needs a priestess, and your parents need you."

Then he's gone towards the Tier. I notice too that he's carrying the black-glass knife in a loop around his waist. It's clean, though I didn't do it.

Ignos shatters the moment, as he often does, with an angry tone.

You're too primitive to answer my questions. To help me remove the block.

I ask Ignos what 'the block' might be, but get no answer.

. . .

As the sky turns purple and orange, I make my way towards the Tier. Some of the crowd is already there, assembled for what promises to be the most interesting sacrifice in some time. Which is when it hits me. I'm performing the ritual, which means I'll have to do the sacrifice. Cut into the man and take out his heart.

I start to sweat. I've never done that before. Even with Father up there, guiding me, the thought of cutting through the living skin of another person is terrifying.

You saw the entire sky light on fire. Picked your way through a dark and dangerous jungle to find something you've never imagined before. Went up to it and met me, and you're scared of something you've seen so many times?

Ignos, of course, is right. This shouldn't be so hard.

That's what I tell myself as I walk between the gathering people to the foot of the Tier. I've climbed up and down these stones before.

Dawn is the best time, when the rocks are cool and at the top you can see the blanket of mist covering the entire jungle. Trees poking their green leaves through. Now the stones are warm and I lift each leg, place each hand slow, taking care to plant my feet correctly. One step at a time. Nobody will trust a priestess that falls.

I glance up and see Father's already up at the top, along with the man blowing the hollowed caller. A sound I don't really hear as I'm so focused on climbing. The sacrifice is there too, along with the usual pair of assisting elders. This one is a scrawny hunter, and unlike yesterday's, his face is full of fear.

You and me both, I want to say, but that would be cruel. He's going to die regardless. I'm only dead if I fail.

Which isn't going to happen.

Ignos is suddenly full of encouragement. As if the god realizes his chosen body might go under the knife if he can't come up with something good. If I misremember a crucial phrase, or botch the cutting.

But I manage the first stage well enough. Make it to the top, next to the altar. Ignos' light is still hot up here, even at dusk. Like he's staring right at me across the horizon, and now I know why Father seems to spend the whole ceremony looking down at us or with his eyes closed. Doing anything else means blindness.

When I angle down to my village, though, I don't see the rows of people I'm looking for. Instead, the crowd is pushing into itself. Cowering against one another, because there's an army—no, that's too big of a word, a patrol—surrounding them. Maybe three dozen. Only these aren't wearing the capes and cloths of our hunters. Many of these sport patchwork brown skins of bears on their heads, and all of them hold weapons.

Kukri. I can catch the black-glass glint from up here. The shards are jammed into the tops of wooden sticks, the glass cut like an eagle's talons. Like the knife Father still holds, they're capable of tearing a person apart. I know because our village has only one, taken from a long-ago prisoner. It sits, unused, in someone's house. Our bows and arrows make for more effective hunting. Nobody would bother with kukri in the jungle.

Which, it hits me, is what these warriors are. They're not Solare. They're from outside, the plains to the West. We call them Charre, and in some distant past they left the jungle behind for clear skies and the brutality that comes when there's no place to hide.

As I'm processing this, one of the Charre, the only one I can see wearing the faded tan furs of a lion around his neck and shoulders, comes forward towards the Tier. Our villagers don't stop him, but shrink back, with mothers putting arms around sons, and fathers moving to shield them both. It's time for the ritual, so nobody is armed. Other tribes wouldn't think of a raid now—showing such disrespect for Ignos would be unthinkable.

Which is why I'm not so surprised when the lion warrior waves at me to carry on. Now that he's closer, I can see that he's not much older than I am, though his chest bears a few scars and his dark arms appear covered in tattoos. He notices my stare and gives me a smile in return, as though I'm supposed to treat their interruption as nothing.

They're here for you.

Ignos says it the same moment I'm piecing it together. Our village isn't the largest, our tribe isn't the wealthiest. The only reason these Charre might come to our little town is because they heard a woman talking about how she communes with their god.

"Begin the ceremony, Kaishi," Father says. "There is no other option, now."

I take a deep breath. Feel the humid jungle air fill my lungs, and when Ignos begins to feed me lines, I say them. One after another. I lose myself in the recitation, so much so that I don't even know what I'm saying. It could have been complete nonsense, except I see the crowd falling into words. Even the Charre turn towards me, let their kukri hang loose in their hands. At the base of the Tier, the lion warrior drops to his knees.

I speak the last line and my voice falls silent. Father moves forward with the knife, and I know right now that I cannot kill this man. I'm not ready, and I don't know how.

"I can't," I whisper, turning and taking the black-glass knife from Father anyway, to hide our voices.

"You must," he replies, though I can tell he's sorry to say so.

I stand over the sacrifice, who now has both elders' hands pinning his back to the altar. His white eyes roll towards me. His lips are drawn back, and I can tell he wants to scream but can't quite bring himself to it. Can't shed that last end of his dignity.

I hesitate.

Give the sacrifice to the Charre. There is no dishonor there, right?

If Ignos himself tells me there is no dishonor, then there cannot be. My relief at the escape pushes me to point the black-glass knife down the steps towards the lion warrior, who starts in surprise.

"We give this honor to you, visitors, so that you may leave our village in peace," I say, using the same words Father has said before, though that was trading trinkets, not whole persons.

The lion warrior covers any shock, sliding on a straight face. He stands, "I came to see a priestess, and I believe I have." The warrior shifts to look at the crowd and I see that his back, too, is tattooed in a black-inked version of Ignos, a dark halo and colored rays shining up to the warrior's shoulders. "Your priestess has bought your survival with the offer of this sacrifice. She can buy your freedom as well, with her own."

Ignos' shock runs through my mind, mingling with mine. Quick enough, though, Father is next to me, whispering in my ear.

"You must go, Kaishi," he's saying. "Do not fight. Do not resist, or they will kill us all and take you anyway."

I had expected Father to deny this warrior's demands. To call my village to fight in my defense, but even as his words churn my stomach I see their point.

I asked Ignos for a destiny and he's delivered.

To save my family, my village, I move down those steps. Go past the lion warrior, and feel him walk behind me. Hear his call to gather the sacrifice and prepare to leave.

He lets me say goodbye to Mother, Father, and I know I'll never see them again.

8 / ASSAULT

The thing about gravity is that, this far from the gas giant, there's not much of it. Only enough to boost the Oratus' momentum. Which works in their favor, because when the shuttle's pointed tip pierces the seed ship's hull, allowing the nose to crash through, Sax and the others let go of the hanging bars and shoot forward towards that translucent shuttle bow.

Where they'll splat into a gooey pile if things don't work as they should.

But the shuttle is a Vincere craft, and the Flaum that maintain it do so with the constant penalty of death for any failure whatsoever. Vigilance isn't just expected, it's enforced. So the shuttle's nose bursts like a blossoming star; pointed triangles flaring out and leaving a wide open window into the seed ship for Sax and the other three to fly through.

For the barest second as he launches from the shuttle, Sax feels the tug of vacuum pulling him back towards space. Then, again, the shuttle does its job: those flared ends fold back against the seed ship's inside hull, and from each one slides out metal slats. They mesh with each other and create a seal against outer space, and now the fun's beginning.

The four Oratus soar into what looks like the seed ship's growth quadrant. Dark blue lights shine from the top of a smooth ceiling down onto open clusters of terminals and liquid-filled tanks that quickly give way to a forest of glass tubes, most full of greenish ooze and the floating bodies of all sorts of species. They're tall, going from floor to ceiling, which in the seed ship means a towering height. Ten times Sax's own. The Oratus have to watch themselves or they'll splatter against those tubes too.

Not that they have much control after being flung out of the shuttle. Sax, with the Stim giving him plenty of time to look as the four of them fly over the Sevora's thin defense, has a second to torque himself around before he hits the first tube.

He tenses his muscles.

And bounces.

His claws slide across the glass, pulling him around the tube and then Sax kicks off, launching himself further towards the back of the section. Bas, Gar, and Lan do the same, jumping from one tube to the next, leaving behind the growing laser-light show as their soldiers engage the Sevora.

Who, it looks like, are using Flaum too. Only these aren't the same as the Vincere soldiers. Mostly because the Vincere conscripts are actually Flaum, all the way through. On the Sevora side, though, they're just bodies. Flaum hands holding the rifles, fingers pulling the trigger, with a Sevora in their heads calling every shot.

Which is why Sax, with every tube he hits, digs his claws in just enough to crack the glass. To splinter it inside the tube and start the fluid spilling. The leak will kill the half-grown specimen inside. Prevent one more Sevora from getting the body it wants. If the mission succeeds, all of these test tube species will die anyway, but Sax prefers confirmed kills to hypothetical ones.

The seed ship's own homespun gravity, coupled with the gas giant's, starts to pull the set down before they've reached the end of the tube forest. Sax calls, through the mask, for his team to drop now so they don't get too scattered, and the next tube he hits serves as his ride to the ground.

At the base, it's a hard metal landing. Terminals whiz and beep as Sax crashes into a deserted cluster of tubes. Monitors show waving lines and green numbers. Sax ignores it all and orients himself towards the back of the section. They have to get further into the seed ship, and they don't have long to do it.

A chittering noise slips in through Sax's mask. Followed by more. Looks like some of the Sevora saw them flying overhead. Weren't fooled by the assault troops spilling from the shuttle. Sax reaches for his own miner and draws it from his belt. The miner is made for an Oratus, with circles that close neatly where each claw ought to go. Precise, deadly control.

Only the chitters aren't coming closer. Maybe Sax is wrong. Maybe they didn't notice.

But now Sax has noticed them.

He creeps around the tubes, careful to place his claws lightly on the metal floor. The soft gravity here means such steps aren't hard. Sax just has to be careful so an accidental twitch doesn't send him floating.

What Sax sees when he pokes his head around the side of a tube cluster and into a wide hallway, is a trio of Sevora Flaum setting up a gouter on a tripod. A large cylinder attached to a pair of wheeled containers as large as Sax, the gouter will, in another moment, start spraying hot chemical doom through the air towards the Vincere troops.

The gouter's liquid would melt a mask in no time, and would melt a hull too, which is why, when it cools, the stuff hardens into a stiff seal. The Sevora don't see Sax, so he takes a moment to put his miner back. No sense wasting energy.

Or fun.

Sax bursts around the corner, claws digging hard into the floor, then he leaps at the Flaum settling in to the gouter's targeting chair. The Flaum's friends turn at the shriek of tearing metal, but all they have time to do is scream before Sax hits. His claws do the work on the gunner, while Sax uses his tail to wrap around the left one's neck.

Constricts enough to feel the jolt that says the job's done, and then he's turning to the last one. Sometimes Sevora know their end is coming, and they face it bravely. Stand there silent as Sax claims them for his kill count. This one, though, cowers. Backs away from the Oratus as Sax climbs out from the gouter's chair. Behind him, Sax uses his tail to bash apart the chemical feeds, ruining the weapon for any future parties.

"Tell me, Sevora," Sax hisses as he towers over the tiny Flaum. "What are you hoping will happen? That I'll spare you because you look so pathetic?"

The Sevora stares back at Sax through the Flaum's big black eyes. There's still a small weapon hanging from the Sevora's holster. If drawn and shot perfectly, it might pierce the mask. Give Sax a scar. Sax wants the Sevora to reach for it, to see if Sax is faster. He doesn't get the chance.

Bas dashes by in front of him, and without breaking stride, her claws leave a fatal rend that has the Sevora collapsing to the ground.

"Stop playing with your food," Bas says through the mask as she hurtles on towards the edge of the section.

Sax can't argue with her logic, and he bounds after her. They're almost to the gate leading further into the seed ship. Which is good, because, by Sax's counting, their time is almost up.

The Charre have grown like a nightmare. I first heard of them years ago, through stories told by passing traders. If we had a penchant for sacrifice, the Charre have an obsession. They feed on conquest. On taking land and people and abusing both. Father would curse them and, in equal breath, our own ancestors for letting Solare fall into such squabbling decline.

When the Lunare appeared, however, everything seemed to change. Caught between two greater powers, Father and the elders held long nights debating about which side to join. Staying independent meant death, of that they were certain. Still, they had pushed back a formal decision, waiting to see which of the two would prove more dangerous.

Now here I am, being pushed through the jungle by kukri-wielding warriors, a victim of that indecision. My anger, though, funnels to the only possible target: the lion-sporting chief who walks next to me while his band spreads out around us.

As we move away from the village, his stance changes. Out of the eyes of the crowd, he relaxes, even presumes to offer me a friendly smile. He's not much older than me, and his frame, as I look at him, says he's a powerful hunter, though every glance is undercut by the fact that he could order me killed should the mood strike.

The shape of his eyes and his smooth skin—he has white-lance scars on his chest and legs, mingling with the tattoos, but his face has been spared—boosts the appeal. He radiates a charm, an ease with the power he holds, but it's nothing against my wall of rage. I'm almost surprised at how angry I am, but the shock of being taken transmutes itself to fire easily.

"My name is Malo," he says, and I nearly spit at his face.

"I don't care," I reply.

You should. His smile looks genuine, and he might be the only friend you have now.

Ignos is right, of course, but I'm human and can't accept the current state of things without flaring up. Malo sees this and swallows, looks around as if hoping one of his warriors will offer an excuse to end the conversation. But he doesn't break stride and stays by my side.

A brave move.

I thought you asked for a destiny? Is this not what you wanted?

Again I cede the point. Why ask for a change if you're going to be devastated when it happens? My counter argument goes like this:

Damn destiny, I want my family back.

"I'm sorry," Malo tries conversation again. "I know it's hard."

"I don't know how you expect this to go," I reply, cooling my heat long enough to form a real sentence. "You took me from my home. You've surrounded me with killers. I'm not going to be your friend."

"I don't need you to be my friend," Malo replies. "I do, however, need you to listen."

That I can do. Listening lets me simmer in my self-pity, and I revel in it while Malo talks about the rules of traveling with a Charre army. When food is served, how sleeping works, and the marching schedule. All of it's aggressive. Dawn to dusk and with expedience. Even the hunters in our tribe don't approach the Charre's hours on the move.

Malo's words lay lightly on my mind as I race through memories of my parents, childhood, and routines that I'm now realizing may be forever gone. Eventually Malo becomes aware that I'm not asking questions or even looking at him—my eyes have drifted to some vague point in front of us—and he stops. Waits for me to ask him to keep going.

I don't, because I'm recalling the pig planted beneath the earth and how, right now, Father is probably taking a bite of it. Part of me hopes he can't eat it after losing his daughter, and another part is ashamed at the same.

"Can you tell me your name?" Malo's question interrupts.

"Kaishi," I say.

"Look around at my warriors and tell me what you see." Malo sweeps his own gaze around the band.

They're not all visible in the night as some are scouting through the brush, but there are at least a dozen around us. I don't expect the question, and that prompts me to follow his suggestion and peer around.

All of the warriors carry weapons and have tattoos. Most wear the giant, toothy maws of bears in the same way Malo sports the lion skin. I see something else, too: many of the warriors are blinking, stepping on roots here and there. Those carrying spears in addition to their kukri have them hanging low rather than at proper marching height.

"They're exhausted," I say, and the breach in the Charre's invincible myth is a comfort.

"We ran all morning and afternoon to reach you," Malo says. "We didn't want to lose time."

"Lose time?"

"Ignos sent a sign, Kaishi. Surely you saw it? A great fire in the sky?"

I nod.

"We were camped north of here, waiting to meet another of our bands, but when we saw where the fire touched the earth, we left to head this way. We ran into one of your village's messengers as we traveled, he was quick to tell us what had happened."

"I went there. To where the fire touched." There doesn't seem to be much point in hiding it. "That's where I found Ignos. He talks to me, and then I say his words."

"Then you are precisely what we need," Malo says. "Whispers float through our cities that hordes from the mountains are coming, and that they have constructs so massive only Ignos himself could have built them. That they hold weapons which can spit fire."

"What does that have to do with me?"

"You are divine, Kaishi." Malo's hands twitch towards me as he says this, as though he wants to grab my shoulders. "At least, if you are telling the truth. What the Emperor needs now is someone to show that Ignos is still with us. To prove that the Lunare are not the chosen people."

As Malo speaks these words, his face transforms and his eyes pick up the same fervor that I saw when he bowed to me at the base of the Tier. He wants to believe me. He wants me to be the miracle his people need.

You can be, Kaishi. They are looking for hope. You can be more than that—you can be real. Keep this one close to you. We can use him.

Use him? The word is oily, somehow, and I recoil from it.

You're naive. Everyone can be used, and to carry out my mission, you will need to use many.

Ignos' mission. Preparing us for a new future. That is more important than any discomfort I might feel over simple terms. So when I realize Malo's staring at me with worry, I do what I can to dispel it.

"Ignos asks me questions sometimes," I say.

"A god asks you questions?"

Malo's point is a good one, but I've come up with my own answer to it already, one that Ignos confirmed when I suggested it hours ago. "He's testing my faith."

Ignos says I should keep Malo close, so I climb the mountain of my rage and seek cool understanding on the summit. "You've seen my home, Malo, tell me about yours?"

This sparks another, different expression from the soldier who I'm starting to think has a thousand faces. His lips turn up at the corners, he looks to some point west, and his mouth opens slightly before he talks, as if measuring the words for their worth. "Have you heard of Damantum?"

The name is familiar, like a minor character in a story often told. I shake my head.

"Then you have missed the greatest city in all the world." Malo's hands start to sweep as he talks. "Damantum covers an island with gold that glitters in the light of Ignos. Lush gardens float on its gentle waters. Markets throng in every street, offering wonders of which you and I can barely imagine."

I'm sure Malo would keep going, but I interrupt him, because there's only so much adoration I can stand, "You sound like the Lunare. She talks of her mountain cities in the same way."

After I say this, I realize Malo likely has no idea who I'm talking about, but, to my surprise, Malo glances behind us. I follow and there, her hands bound but feet moving free, flanked by two warriors, marches Viera.

"Unlike the Lunare, what I speak of is true," Malo says. "When we reach Damantum, you will understand."

"Why did you bring her?"

"To see if, underneath her boasts and lies, we may learn something of her brethren," Malo says. "And once we do, her sacrifice will be a glorious one." He looks at me, the fervor returning to his face. "I hope you will wield the knife."

10 / THE GATEWAY

The far end of the first section is marked by a gateway; a broad arch bordered by soft green globes spaced every couple of meters. Every seed ship is made up of twelve sections split by these gateways, and getting through them before the Sevora lock the gates is imperative.

Bas reaches the gateway first after scaling the twenty shallow, flat steps leading up to the door. As she does so, with Sax coming hot behind her, those soft green globes flip to a bright red. They'd taken too long, and now every second spent on this side of the gateway would give the Sevora time to organize a defense on the other side.

To the right, next to a red globe at Sax's chest level, there's a black protrusion. Like a bulb, only opaque.

"Mind scanners," Lan says as she and Gar join them on the landing. Sax notes that Gar's mid-claws, like his own, are red and wet.

"Unless one of you has managed to get infected, we're not getting this gateway open."

"I tried," Sax offers. "But they died too quickly."

"Good," Gar replies. "Because I would tear you apart if they hadn't."

"I would like to see you try." Sax opens his mouth slightly, shows row after row of razor teeth.

"Cutters," Bas interrupts, and she completes the interruption by stepping between Gar and Sax. "We burn our way through."

That's all she needs to say. The four of them pull small canisters with smaller tubes attached at right angles around them. They each stick their claws into the tops of those tubes and push down, mixing the volatile gasses, while the claw holding the weapon clicks the release.

Lightning-blue beams spit out from the ends and slam into the gateway. Their fire concentrates on a small section, tracing out a square for them to fit through. The cutters are so bright that Sax can't stare right at them, but instead at the curling, blackened bits of metal falling to the floor beneath.

In the distance, behind them, there's the sound of equipment exploding. Bangs and pops signaling the destruction of seed ship gear. The Vincere forces have won the first battle, and too quickly. Victory means whatever Sevora forces remain will be retreating right towards the four of them.

"Bas, trade you," Sax says, handing his cutter to his pair, who gives him her miner. The motion causes a brief blip in the burning, but the delay is worth it.

None of them wants to catch a laser bolt to the back.

Malo doesn't halt the march until the jungle canopies disappear and stars shine. I've seen stars from our clearings, of course, but it's my first time this far west and having an entire horizon splashed in Nomis' glow stops me.

We're at the head of a valley that, after days and days of hiking, should lead us to the volcano that marks the true base of Charre territory. Malo's laid out the course for me, and while I'm excited at seeing someplace new, every step takes me away from familiarity.

Which is why, lying down on my cotton mat, placed over the rock-sand ground, I'm not able to fall asleep. The desert has its own sounds, but they're not the ones I know. Monkeys and owls aren't calling, the whistle of wind through the trees is missing, and even the insects buzz differently.

Though, I notice, they still bite.

The Charre replace the noises I know with clanking, chopping ones. Cook fires spring up, though I tell Malo I'm not hungry. Truth is, I don't know if I am or not—everything is too much right now. So I stay there on the thin mat, feel the rocks dig into my back, and talk to Ignos.

You tell me these Charre are greatly feared?

As much as any one group can be, I suppose. Fear, I think, might be the wrong word. It doesn't do us much good to be afraid in the jungle because there are so many ways things can go bad. Rather, I would say the Charre, of all people, are the ones most likely to destroy what we have. If that is fear, then yes, we fear them.

And yet, they seem to value you.

It's not me they care about. It's him. Ignos is who they're looking for.

But they believe you. Malo does, at least. He's your path to power.

Power for what?

Anything. Once you have the resources, that bracelet on your wrist will give you everything you could ever need.

I look at the Cache, but it's not much now. A simple thing sitting on my arm. It doesn't flash, or whisper secrets in my mind. I try to will it to do something. Tell it to light up.

"Work," I say to it.

"Who are you talking to?" Malo asks, sitting down beside me.

Before I respond, he hands me a bundle of maize in a thin tortilla.

"I said I wasn't hungry." I take it anyway and Malo smiles.

"Everyone's hungry after a hike like that. I can't have you tired tomorrow. It's going to be a long walk."

The food is bland, but my stomach likes it fine and I devour the whole thing in three bites. Malo even has a skin of water for me, and I squeeze some out into my mouth. It's warm, stale, and delicious.

After I'm done, Malo takes the skin back and notices I'm looking at his hands. Trying to see if he brought more. He laughs. I can't help but crack a small smile too. Then Malo's up and away, back a second later with another tortilla. This one, along with the maize, has bits of meat in it. I recognize the iguana, though the strange green circles scattered throughout are new to me.

"Take it in small bites," Malo says. I don't really listen and take a third of the tortilla in a single chomp.

The warmth comes slow, but it builds into incredible heat. The insides of my mouth burn, and as my eyes go wide, Malo hands me a small bowl full of a light orange juice. I drain the whole thing, the mango sweetness staving off the feeling that I'm about to die right there.

What are you doing? Did he poison you? Why are you burning?

I suck in mouthfuls of air, and then I notice Malo is laughing again.

"A little bit at a time, priestess."

I note the title and wonder if that's going to be me from now on.

The priestess.

Focusing on that does more than the mango juice to quiet the burn, and, as my mouth calms down, I find myself reaching for the tortilla again. Malo holds it away.

"You'll take it slow this time?" Malo says and I nod.

I'm true to my word, and, with little bites of fire, I finish the tortilla. When I'm done, Malo's expression is more serious than I'd expected.

"What's wrong?" I say.

"You'll have to learn to like the peppers," Malo says, and I can tell this isn't a casual conversation any more. "In Damantum, you'll eat with priests. Maybe even the Emperor. They will look for signs Ignos isn't with you. That you're lying. No priestess of the Charre will refuse our own food."

"Everyone likes these in Damantum? I'll be doubted because of a pepper?"

"By those who fear your power, yes. I've seen many of my own warriors placed on the altar because the priests found some way they had displeased Ignos." Malo's annoyed, and this is the first time I really see why he's the leader here. "There are those in Damantum who would trample over anyone in their path. We have days ahead of us, priestess. If you would like, I want to use our evenings to teach you how to survive in my city."

I don't need Ignos' advice to say yes to that one, and shortly after Malo vanishes into the night, saying we should both get what sleep we can. Except now I'm thinking about the den of snakes I'm walking into and it's enough to keep my mind churning.

I hear laughter not far off. I roll over on the mat and look and there's the Lunare, Viera, talking with a pair of Charre around their fire. They've unbound her arms, which means they must think she's not a threat. Viera's in the middle of some story, and her hands are waving around, her ragged clothes looking ridiculous, and I can see why the Charre don't think she'll cause any harm.

But you don't agree. Why?

Because the Lunare have a history. Because they trade, yes, but they also take. The Solare, what tribes we have left, have been squeezed between the Charre to the West and the Lunare in their mountains to the East. Oceans cover the other two directions, trapping us. Father believes Ignos will save those of us who are left, and I believe him. I do. But we're running out of time.

You didn't answer my question, Kaishi.

Why is Viera dangerous? Because I know what the Lunare leave behind when they raid a tribe. The burned-out corpses with dark holes in their bodies. Houses torn apart and looted. Anyone not dead is, we think, taken away. To what end, we don't know.

I don't think Viera's like the others—I'd even call her my friend but Father's warned me enough times that she's going to bring trouble that I can't dismiss it entirely.

Then why do your tribes not band together and strike? Defend and attack as one?

It's not like the Solare haven't tried. It's not like my father and the elders haven't met with other tribes and talked of an alliance. Every time he returns with a shaking head and grumbles of power, and how hard it is to give up a little, even in the face of losing it all forever. So we trade what we can with the Lunare and hope they'll leave us alone.

Then why don't you try something different?

I look over at the fire and Viera, still chattering. It doesn't take much thought to see where Ignos is going with this, and I'm not tired yet anyway, so I sit up from my mat and, after pulling my mosswrap around me to cut the chill night breeze, head over towards their fire.

The Charre warriors glance at me as I approach and the simultaneous moving of those big, brown bear heads and their gleaming teeth swinging in my direction makes me pause. They won't hurt me, I tell myself, because if they'd wanted to have me dead, it would have happened before dinner. No sense wasting food on a body.

"Hearing my stories?" Viera speaks to me. "How do they match up? Figure a priestess has to have some good ones of her own."

The flames give her face a luminous glow, and the shadows play between her large eyes and the wisps of snow-white hair playing down her forehead. Interrupted, Viera's hunching over the fire, as though she's trying to hug the flames. Before I ask how she can stand the heat, Viera straightens, turns, and leans her back over the burning brush.

"Are you cold?" I ask, ignoring her question.

I have stories. Plenty. We've swapped some during our jungle runs.

"You see the snow on top of the mountains?" Viera replies, and I note that she's talking in Solare tongue. "You probably think it's cold for us. That we should be used to it?"

The warriors return to watching Viera with quirked smiles, and I realize that they don't understand a word of what the Lunare is saying. They're laughing because holding one's self over a fire looks ludicrous. I'm so used to both languages that swapping between Charre and Solare tongues comes as naturally as breathing.

"But we go deep," Viera continues. "Our pathways hollow so far that we catch the heat of the world. It's like this fire here, but everywhere and all the time. So yes, I'm cold."

I take my own seat near the fire. The sand is warm on my legs, soft and smooth. Straight back the way we came, beyond the camp, the jungle trees dance in the breeze. The Lunare live deep in the mountains. I can't imagine what it would be like to not see the sky, and turn away from the thought.

"They can't understand you," I say, and it takes a second for Viera to realize that I'm talking about the warriors.

"You can't understand me?" Viera says the words in Solare and the warriors greet the phrase with blank stares. "Interesting. I guess that means I can spend all day insulting them and nobody will know."

"I will," I say.

"Yes, you will," Viera says the reply slowly and sits back from the fire, looking at me. "Why'd you come over here, Kaishi? Lonely?"

"Because you were talking so loudly I couldn't get to sleep."

"It's a habit of mine." Viera shrugs. "Is this a warning? Is Ignos going to strike me down if I don't let his priestess rest?"

The casual blasphemy bites my ears, and I'm about to scold her for it when Ignos rushes through my mind.

Look past the flaws to what she can bring us, Kaishi. I will forgive anything said against me so long as you achieve my goal.

Ignos makes sense, so I give Viera a toothy smile, "He might, if I ask him to."

Viera laughs at this, and it's a bouncing, joyful thing. How she can make such a sound in a situation like this is beyond me. When Viera looks my way again, her green-yellow eyes are shining with mirth.

"I thought I would be stuck with dead-eyed warriors," Viera says. "I'm happy they took you along, Kaishi."

"Happy? How can you be happy surrounded by enemies?" I blurt out the question, because there's nothing in the Lunare's tone that speaks of sarcasm.

Viera is, as far as I can tell, genuinely enjoying herself.

"Do you know why I stayed behind when my people returned to the mountains?" Viera asks and I shake my head. "Because of these." The Lunare points to the sky and the starry tapestry. "They're beautiful. So much more so than the rock ceilings that have kept my nights company for so long."

"The stars won't walk for you," I say. "And I don't think these warriors will mind leaving you behind."

"Then I think we'll have to work together, Kaishi," Viera says. "This isn't just another jungle run. It's an adventure, one I think you've been waiting for. I know I have."

"I just want to go home."

"You won't, Kaishi." Viera's smile falls away.

"Why?"

"I love the stars, Kaishi, and so do most of the Lunare. We like your jungle, and we like these sandy plains." Viera takes a long breath, savoring the air. "Visiting is nice. Trading is better. But why stop there?"

"What do you mean?"

"We're coming, Kaishi, and we're going to take everything you and your people have."

Sax sets himself up atop the landing and waits for targets. There's no cover up here, but Sax has options. Moments later, the first scrambling Sevora—Flaum and Whelks, because both Sevora and the Vincere value prodigious breeders—come into view. Some of them pause at the sight of Sax, two are brave enough to reach for weapons.

Sax leaps. Presses his legs against the landing and launches himself straight up. Gravity is light enough that he doesn't simply fall back down, but floats. This, with the Stim, gives him plenty of time to aim. To roast, with red and yellow blasts of energy from his miner, the two initial threats and, quickly enough, more. They burst into burning confetti, superheated by Sax's miners, and soon enough the Sevora rethink their withdrawal.

They scatter back into the tube forest as Sax returns to the ground. He doesn't think there's another way out of this section, so they'll be back, but the soft bang behind him means Sax won't be here to greet them.

Which makes them the lucky ones.

Sax feels a touch on his tail. Familiar. Bas's way of saying 'let's go'. Sax keeps his eyes backward, looking towards their shuttle and any further Sevora attacks while Bas, keeping her tail on his, guides the Oratus through the hole they've cut in the gateway. Only when he's ducked through does Sax turn and look at the section they've entered.

If the last one held the tubes growing the species, this one holds their next stop. It's composed of wide purple-black pools. Each one as large or more than the shuttle Sax and the others came in on. The pools aren't quiet either; they burble and churn with movement beneath the surface.

Gar doesn't wait. He lifts his cutter, aims it towards the nearest pool, and fires. The pool itself heats up, begins to boil with the amount of energy pouring into it. There's a big reason this is a bad idea: the cutters are their best way through the gateways, and there's at least two more before the seed ship's center. Wasting energy on immature Sevora that'll die anyway if the mission succeeds is stupid.

But Sax waits a few moments before ordering Gar to stop. He knows how satisfying this is. He wants to do it himself, but Bas still has his cutter.

"When the ship falls, you'll get them all," Sax says as the cutter's light dies out.

"This is more fun," Gar replies, and they all hiss in knowing agreement.

The pools are criss-crossed by catwalks. Railed bridges spotted with feeding stations and consoles showing temperature and concentrations of minerals Sax neither knows nor cares about. They walk on by, occasionally swiping with claw or tail to break things to pieces.

Pointless, nourishing destruction.

I twist and turn the rest of the night after Viera's warning. The Lunare are coming? With the Charre pressing from the other side, my tribe wouldn't last long. Neither would any of the Solare.

Unless you find an ally.

Ignos makes a good point. If we pressed ourselves into the service of one side or the other, we might survive. It would mean giving up our independence, but I'm not so naive that I believe we're keeping that anyway.

Why are you here, Kaishi?

The question comes with a hint of more. Ignos does this from time to time; makes asks designed to lead me to other conclusions. I don't mind it much, but here in the early morning, tired, with my god beginning to brighten the Eastern sky, I'm not that patient and go with the obvious answer:

I'm here because the Charre came and stole me away from my family and my home.

No, you're here because you have an opportunity.

If Ignos had been my mother, or another village elder, I would have laughed. Pushed the suggestion away. But there's only so much defiance one can have in the face of their god. So I stay quiet and wait for Ignos to continue.

At least some of these warriors believe in you. Malo, the leader, certainly does. Together, we can turn them, Kaishi. Together, we can make them all believe in you.

And then what? I tell them to leave my people alone? How long till they decide I'm not much use as a priestess and tear me apart?

If they believe you are a goddess, they will not touch you.

There's a new word. One that at once makes clear Ignos's plans for me and spawns a thousand questions about why, why bother with a random Solare girl when there are already people—the Charre's Emperor, say—who hold the positions of power Ignos is clearly looking for.

Because you found me, Kaishi.

There are easy rebuttals to this, but I don't have time to make them because Malo and his warriors are calling for the march to start. I scramble and put on my mosswrap. I'm about to start rolling the mat up when a warrior appears, gently pushes me away, and proceeds to take care of my gear.

I insist that I'm capable of handling my own stuff and the warrior just laughs. Puts the mat inside a pack harness looped over his shoulders, and walks off. I follow, because nobody's telling me what to do and I don't want to get left behind.

The Charre move quick in the early morning, despite sore muscles from the day before. At least, I'm guessing everyone feels the same knots and spasms as I do. Malo says we have to cover as much ground as possible before Ignos gets high and the heat makes travel difficult. I say that it's plenty difficult already and the chief gives me a smile.

For some reason, Malo's look makes me flush. I resolve not to let that happen anymore.

. . .

Ignos serves as a distraction. He's badgering me with questions and ideas. Thoughts on how to wrap the Charre around my finger. Musings on what we can do when we have their loyalty. The things we can command them to build. That's where Ignos really gets strange, because the structures he's describing don't exist.

Not that I've seen, anyway.

We're walking through a vast valley whose sandstone cliffs rise up on either side of us. In the far distance is the vague outline of the volcano. Around that, according to our village traders, begin the vast fields and meadows that make up the bulk of Charre territory. Stories whisper about how it used to be forest, but the Charre took the trees for their own ends.

Several hours in, with Ignos getting close to straight over our heads, a call comes from the rear of our column. Malo leaves me behind and pushes through his own warriors to get a better look.

While I can't see over their heads, an expanding dust cloud from back the way we came makes it clear something's heading this way.

"They're running fast," Viera, appearing next to me, says. "Think it's your tribe coming after you?"

The question spins me for a moment. My village does have hunters. They could move fast through the jungle. I want to believe that Father has ordered an all-out attack to get me back.

"He wouldn't do that," I say, dousing the shock of hope in cool logic. "Father wouldn't risk the village for me."

I don't believe it until I say the words, but it's true. Father and Mother kept no secrets about the sacrifices of power. How they had to make decisions against their own interests if the village required it.

What choice would be more obvious than letting their entire tribe survive by losing a single girl?

The rest of Malo's force goes to set up. They form a staggered line, all twenty of them, and begin to pull out their bows and arrows. Their kukri. Viera and I move over to the side, to get a clear look at what's coming our way.

Whomever they are, they're moving at a full sprint. I see their bodies, obscured by dust, pounding forward with arms raised and clubs held high. Their skin makes it clear they're not Viera's kin, the colors of their tattoos clear they're not mine. This is a batch of Solare intent on their own demise.

"Stay back here," Malo slips to us with another warrior by his side. "We're not risking you on a pointless fight."

"Pointless?" the Charre warrior says. "For you, Malo, it may be. The rest of us still need to earn our lions."

"Not at the cost of the priestess," Malo fires back, and then he's gone; returning to the line with his kukri drawn and ready.

"Who are they?" I ask, because I can't believe a Solare tribe would leave the jungle for a fight like this.

"They wish revenge," the warrior says, and I can see the slight smile on his stone face. "We took what we needed from their village days ago. At the time, it was lightly defended. Now, we know why."

I can imagine. Hunters often take days to pursue valuable game. A single large boar, bear, or elephant could feed a village for a long time, but if you were gone when enemies came along, you could lose everything.

"Draw!" Malo's command rings sharp in the clear air. As one, ten of the Charre warriors lift their bows and bend back their strings. "Aim!"

Their angles. Why?

Ignos is noticing that the Charre point their arrows low. To me, it's obvious: less likely to kill your target from their direction.

For the sacrifices. I see.

Again the gaps in Ignos' knowledge seem strange to me, but in the chaos of the coming fight, I can't focus on that. Instead, I see the Charre launch their arrows. They fly towards the gritty and grizzled bodies of tribesmen which I do not recognize, but know anyway as fellow Solare.

There's no sound when the arrows hit except for screams. Those that dodge strikes, whether through luck or by darting to one side, make shouts of their own. Pain and fury mingling together. It's enough to make me hold my breath.

I realize I want the Solare to win.

I know they won't.

The Charre quickly put truth to my thought. They wade forward in a line, exchanging bows for kukri—one in each hand—and, as the Solare close with their clubs and knives, begin a brutal dance. I've never seen a fight before, and I'm horrified by it.

The Charre hook their enemies with the kukri and throw them to the ground, or spin the Solare so that any retaliation swings well wide of its mark. Every time a Solare hits the ground, a Charre is quick to kick away their weapon or, if the Solare refuses to give in, if they try to push themselves back up, the Charre puts the blunt end of the kukri to work.

Malo stands out. He's easy to track with his lion skin, and the chieftain puts himself in the center of the fray. Where the other Charre use their kukri as weapons, Malo wields his as limbs. He whirls and ducks, jabs and counters, turns a club swinging towards his head into a wild miss that leaves its owner open for a hard kick to the knees.

As short as the fight is, the Solare have time to realize they stand no chance against Malo, and by the end he is standing alone amid a pile of surrendering bodies.

Watch yourself.

Ignos whips me away from the spectacle and I see a Solare, one of a few still standing, cutting towards us. He's holding a black-glass knife, a sacrificial instrument turned into a desperate weapon, and I can see tears streaking his face as he moves. The Charre warrior guarding us shifts to plant himself in the Solare's path, and I wait for the inevitable end.

The crack shocks me to my core, and I feel my heart jump. I'm on the ground in an instant, hands covering my ringing ears. The Charre warrior joins me, though he's looking back towards where the noise came from. He doesn't see what I do. He doesn't see the Solare now on suddenly-red ground.

Interesting. There's more to your world than I thought.

I don't know what Ignos means by that. Instead of thinking about it, I follow the Charre warrior's eyes and look behind me. To where Viera stands, holding her gray tube, her pistol. Viera catches me looking, but this time there's no offered nod. No quirk of a smile. She's deadly serious, and so are the Charre warriors—Malo included—who stop tying their new captives to consider the threat.

"Translate for me, Kaishi," Viera says.

She's still holding the pistol. I didn't see what it did, but I've seen the results, so I nod.

"What you just saw can happen again. Will happen again, if I want it to. You'll keep your hands off me, and you'll keep your hands off her, and we'll all make it to your city alive. Understand?"

She's realized you're her only hope of survival. Clever.

I say the words, and the Charre look to Malo for guidance. The lion warrior steps over the bodies and heads straight for Viera. There's a look to him that says harm is coming, and Viera sees it.

Raises the pistol.

Malo stops.

"Don't," I say, though I'm not sure who I'm saying this to. I only know that I've seen enough violence.

"Priestess," Malo speaks to me in Charre. "This Lunare is a risk. A danger. I cannot let her remain."

But you cannot let her leave. Viera has tied herself to you, now. And they fear her. She'll be useful.

"Viera," I say. "Promise me that you won't hurt anyone unless they come after you first."

"Only time I was going to use it anyway." Viera doesn't look at me as she says this, instead matching stares with Malo, who turns to me.

"Then anyone she kills is your responsibility, priestess," Malo says.

In my mind, I feel Ignos' warm approval.

14 / SEPARATION

At the back end of the section, a shorter walk than the first but still minutes, the four of them stare at another gate.

Soft red globes again.

"Cutters," Bas announces and they reach for the weapons.

"Wait." Sax eyes the mind scanner on the gateway's right side. "I have a better idea."

Before any of the others can comment, Sax turns around and jumps into the nearest pool. The light vanishes instantly beneath the surface, but the mask adapts. The suit covers Sax's eyes, and begins feeding a different type of visual information. Red-yellow glows wherever it detects heat. Sevora, swimming in their natural habitat.

Without a host, Sevora are small. One could fit in Sax's palm. They're thin ovals, with numerous tendrils coming out of their larger end. Each of those tendrils is coated in barbed flagella. Useful for climbing, tearing their way inside something.

If a Sevora could get inside Sax's head, he'd be its slave. Its unthinking host. The Sevora know that too, and they swarm him. The mask makes it seem like Sax's whole world is covered in red and yellow. But the mask is pulling double-duty here. The barbs can't pierce it, so the squid creatures flail at Sax uselessly for a second before realizing, while they can't take the Oratus, he *can* take them.

Sax swipes with his claws and grabs a pair of Sevora. Makes his way out of the pool.

Mind scanners are simple things. Looking for signs of a Sevora and that's all. They're not smart enough to know that the Sevora sitting in Sax's claw isn't where its supposed to be. So the scanner makes a chirp and the gateway blinks green. Slides up into the wall.

Sax turns and launches the two Sevora behind him, arcing them out over the pools. Doesn't wait to see if they make a splash or have a harder landing, because the seed ship suddenly lurches. A shuddering jerk, and Sax digs his claws into the floor to keep from falling over. Loud pops follow the shift; echoing their way along the section's walls and coming towards them.

"Go!" Sax yells as explosions follow the pops, breaking apart the section's wall around the gateway.

Vincere conditioning teaches them to follow commands without hesitation precisely for situations like this, where moments make the difference between life and a cold, long death. Sax leaps ahead, with Bas alongside him—Gar and Lan are already gone, but pairs wait for their partner—and they get through the gateway before it slams shut again. This time, not just with the standard door but with a second, thicker one.

On the other side, booms and bangs continue to ripple through the section they were just in. Tearing it apart. There's a gravity tweak then as the seed ship adjusts its rotation to account for the loss of mass. For the fact that the entire two sections Sax and the others went through have separated, taking the rest of the Vincere forces and who knows how many Sevora with them.

And leaving the four Oratus alone. One set against a seed ship full of thousands wanting them dead.

Good odds.

15 / BURY THE DEAD

As the price for leaving Viera her weapon, Malo and the other Charre give Viera its consequences: the corpse of the Solare fighter. Viera stares at it, then looks at me.

"When people die in Lunare," Viera says. "We cast them off the cliffs. Nature takes care of the bodies after that."

"There are no cliffs here," I reply. "Ignos asks that we burn our bodies, to bring his fallen back to him."

I'm hoping Viera will understand, because I'm having a hard time looking at the graying corpse. True, conflicts between Solare tribes often ended with dead, but they were marked by the stains and stabs of spears and arrows. This one, this one appears dead by magic. I don't want to turn him over, to see what Viera's weapon has done.

"Then we'll burn him."

Viera doesn't have a fire to steal from, but it's not hard to gather enough scrub brush from the scraggly bushes littering the area. I help her, partly for the distraction of using my own hands.

Behind us, the Charre finish up with their captives. Malo gives notice that it's a short time till we march again. He seems entirely willing to leave us behind.

"I don't think your Charre friend is happy with you," Viera says as we pile up the brush.

"I don't care if he is," I reply.

That's not true though. I do want Malo to like me, and not just because Ignos tells me his support will be important. For what, I'm still not sure. If my god demands it of me, however, who am I to deny his wishes?

"You don't?" Viera laughs. "The way you're looking at him says otherwise."

She takes the black-glass knife the Solare was carrying and begins striking it against a small rock. Every hit brings sparks that flash into our brush. No fire yet, though.

"Just how am I looking at him?"

"In Lunare, we have an expression for this. We call it 'shining' when one spots another they desire." Viera keeps whacking with the black-glass blade.

"You think I'm 'shining' Malo?" I feel my way around the word and instantly dislike it. It's not something the Solare would say.

"You might not know it yet," Viera replies, and as she does so, one of the sparks finally catches. The brush goes up in orange, and suddenly there's heat on my face to match Ignos' burning light against my back. "But you are. Nothing to be ashamed of. He's wearing a lion. Enough to make anyone look at him twice."

I search for a long stick to bring the fire to the body and realize, here in the desert, that there are none. Only bushes. Small twigs. My attempt to storm away from Viera's questions ends in failure, and I look away from her as she stands. Try to find somewhere to go.

"We'll have to pull him over," Viera moves on from our conversation, though what she says repulses me.

I've never touched a dead body before, but Viera needs someone to pull the other hand, and the Charre aren't going to help. The Solare's fingers are cool to the touch—I imagine they would be colder if not for Ignos' work—but they're easy to grip. I plant my feet and it's like hauling grain, or pulling on a cart.

Only this one used to be alive.

We get the Solare to the fire, but I'm not sorry we don't get to see the results of our work. Malo's pressing us to move, and I'm eager to find somewhere out of the heat. Viera doesn't say another word as we rejoin the march, and I wonder if she's thinking, looking at all the Solare captives that survive, whether killing one was the right move.

She staked out her power. See how the others watch Viera warily now? You ought to find something similar, so they see you as a threat.

I'm a Solare daughter without her tribe, in a place I don't know. I'm the opposite of a threat.

Remember the Cache. It can help you.

I'd almost forgotten about the bracelet. It's still on my wrist, the same green-brown it's always been. I ask Ignos if it can make something like Viera's gray tube appear.

It can do far better. We can use it to show the Charre, when the time is right, that they should not only fear you, but obey you. Then, you can prepare them for the coming of their gods. Of yours too.

Their escape is manifest in more ways than one: the section they've entered now, unlike the first two, is lit in creamy white, and it's clear the Sevora inside it aren't operating any sort of defense. Sax is stunned to see no weapons aimed their way.

No shouts or shots zinging into their masks. In fact, aside from their set, the landing is empty.

The rest of the section is not, though there are no glowing tubes and only one small purple-black pool that Sax can make out. The flat steps leading down from the landing hit what looks like soft blue rubber with even lines sectioning it into lanes. The rubber itself looks gouged, with deep scars crisscrossing its surface.

The track rings the entire section, and all the divisions within it. There are arenas with stacks of equipment—weights and bars. Target ranges where, even now, Sax can see a trio of Flaum sending hot lasers into thin hit slips.

In the center of the section stands a quad set of buildings, reaching three stories high and sporting flat roofs. Square, open-air windows dot them at precise intervals.

"I forget that the Sevora live here too," Lan says, and Sax agrees.

A Vincere station wouldn't be all that different, really.

"Why aren't they looking for a fight?" Gar asks.

"The separation is the last resort," Bas answers. "They would not split away a whole section unless there were no other option. So perhaps they think we were caught inside it?"

"We need to get to cover," Sax interrupts.

They have, somehow, regained the advantage of surprise and he doesn't want to lose it standing in plain view.

As they limber down to the track, then walk across onto the first pathway they find, Sax realizes there's no cover to be found. Thin fences separate the arenas, more, Sax suspects, for safety than for security. The barriers don't hide their massive Oratus bodies, and at least one of the Sevora must have seen them by now.

So why aren't they attacking?

"I'll take the lead," Gar says.

Nobody argues this and Sax puts himself at the rear, still puzzling.

"Go quick, straight for the gate," Lan says as they form their line. "I'm not sure what's going on, but let's take advantage."

"No." Sax thinks he has the idea. "Be calm. Move slow. Don't fire your weapons. Let's see how they react."

Gar, for once, listens. They walk, claws hanging loose with weapons sheathed. The experience makes Sax itch; he's not one for stealth. An Oratus is made for destruction, not sneaking. Intelligence gathering fell squarely into Flaum territory. When a group of the furry creatures—all, given by their precise motions and lack of chittering conversation, infected with Sevora—passes by them, it's all Sax can do not to reach out and tear them apart.

But it's that nonchalant passing that gives Sax the proof he needs to confirm his theory: the idea of hostiles this far into the seed ship is so strange that the Sevora believe the four of them are hosts. That the Oratus have been taken and they're simply moving about the ship like the rest of the infected.

What's more disturbing to Sax is that, if the Sevora think this, then they must have evidence. It's the greatest shame, the worst possible thing for an Oratus to allow themselves to be taken by a Sevora. If trapped, self-slaughter is a last resort. The preferred way is to die taking as many enemies as possible down with you. Capture... the thought has Sax opening his mouth to hiss before he remembers what they're doing and closes it again.

Never. Sax would die a thousand deaths before the Sevora take him.

The volcano's name is Tutio, Malo tells me. To the Charre, it's a symbol of their own survival. We're looking at the puffs of smoke rising from Tutio's snow-ringed top as we devour our last breakfast before making the final march to Damantum. The city's there, down the slope to my left, where the sands of the desert give way to brown, wavy fields.

"Survival?" I ask, because Solare stories say to stay as far away from Tutio as possible. The volcano has a habit of getting angry, and those who don't respect that anger tend to succumb to it.

"Yes." Malo speaks in his reverent tone again, the one that comes up every time he discusses the Charre's god, Damantum, or, really, anything about Charre life. "Many times Tutio has burned Damantum to the ground. Razed our fields with its furies. You would think this a bad thing, right?"

"Generally."

"At first, of course, it is. People die in the fires, and those that don't might starve. Eventually, though, the Charre return. We build stronger walls and deeper trenches to catch Tutio's liquid flame. The fields that come back are larger and healthier than before. We grow, Kaishi."

This is a ridiculous view. No civilization grows stronger by having itself destroyed routinely. Yet another thing we will change, Kaishi.

I agree with Ignos, though I'm not so sure about his comment on change. Even if I get to some level of power where I can demand things of the Charre, I doubt I'll be able to get them to move their city.

No, we will stop the volcano itself.

Malo notices my mouth hang open and cocks his head. "Are you all right, Kaishi? Did my story disturb you?"

I get myself back. "No. Ignos is whispering some strange things."

"What is he saying? Can you tell me?"

I stand, shaking my head. I'm not going to start spilling Ignos' statements to Malo quite yet. Not till I understand them myself. The only reason I'm alive is that Malo thinks I'm talking to a benevolent god. If he thinks Ignos wants to dominate his civilization, that tone might change.

I wonder, then, why I care? At the start of the march, way back in the jungle, I'd been sulking. Dismal. If the Charre had decided at the end of that first day that keeping me along was a burden too heavy to carry, I'm not sure I would have fought them.

Now I see Malo watching me with a mix of questions and concerns, and I'm... not happy, but alive and glad to be so. Even if Ignos is Malo's main concern, it's nice knowing he cares about me. At least a little.

Viera, too. In the day since we burned the body, the Lunare has left my side only for natural reasons and when I've asked her to.

She's otherwise walking next to me, sharing stories of her home-land beneath the rocks. Her endless legends cover everything from massive monsters making new caves of their own to a week-long cele-bration when the snow melts and all of Lunare has more water than they can drink.

In short, I have friends. Not something I had back home, when people saw me as the priest's daughter. Someone to be respected, yes, but not befriended, lest any offense you caused brought the wrath of Ignos upon you.

Damantum sprawls in the distance ahead of me. Unlike my village, which spread haphazard through jungle clearings, this city is ordered. Wide avenues split rectangular districts, and the river circling Damantum is bridged in several places by arching stonework. To the northeast, the plains give way to blue ocean.

I focus on a sloped building in the center of Damantum. It's hard not to look at it, because the structure appears to be gold. Ignos blazes out from its surface, so that I find myself shading my eyes, trying to get a better look.

"The Vaos," Malo says, joining my watch. "It's the center of Damantum, and the greatest thing the Charre have ever made. Even Tutio dares not destroy it."

"What is it for?" I ask, and Malo looks at me with another one of those nice smiles.

"You, Kaishi. It's for you."

They've made it to the buildings and now Sax sees that these are rooms of a different type. Large, enclosed spaces with pitch-black floors, walls, and ceilings. He sees these through the building on his left, while the one on the right appears to have its windows covered by sliding shutters. Virtual training.

Complete blackouts in the room, and then projectors give the students whatever they're looking to study. Battles, sure, but Sax remembers even normal lessons buttressed by holographic trips to the subject, whether it was a place or the inside of a body. So many lessons before he earned his first mask.

They go past the buildings and all the way beyond a second set of fenced areas. One in particular draws Sax's eye: a large, mottled spire with various colored bulbs hanging from different heights. Pole-like creatures cluster around and on it. As Sax watches, the poles, through small holes, appear to sprout many-fingered hands that push them around or scuttle them up and down the spire. Tevens.

Supposedly, the hard-shell pole comes from secretions the creatures make, and each one's markings tell the secret of that Teven's ancestry. What Sax really cares about, though, is how something tastes, and Tevens are bland, and the pole shards scratch Sax's throat if they're not properly chewed. There is better food.

At the back of the section they cross the track again, make their way up the steps, and there's another gateway. Red-rimmed like the others. Sax doesn't have a Sevora handy, and pulling out their cutters would ruin any hint of deception they've got going.

"I say we do it anyway," Gar announces when it's clear what they're all thinking. "Look at them down there. This isn't a military force. By the time we cut through, they'll barely have noticed."

"Except they don't know we're here now," Bas says. "If we can get through without them knowing, we could make it to the core undetected."

"Which isn't any fun," Gar replies.

"Sometimes there are more important things than your blood-lust," Lan says, and, after a second, Gar's tail twitches to the floor in agreement.

"So we need someone to let us through," Sax says. "A hostage."

"I've never taken one before," Lan replies. "Always easier to eat a captive."

Truth.

While they've been walking through the section, above the shouts and high-pitched squeal of laser-fire, there's been a constant under-tone of pattering. Soft thuds on the ground. Looking from the landing, Sax identifies the source: a group of circular creatures bolting around the track.

Rotams. A bundle of double-kneed legs around a central round body. The scars on the track have an answer now: every Rotam leg ends in a hard hoof, one that has a retractable claw. Sax has seen Rotam charges before—they wheel up and around every surface, then roll over you, carving you to pieces in the process.

They're eyeless, and sense movement, and sound, through soft fibers coating their body.

Which means Sax can wait, down by the track, for the Rotam to pass by. As long as the Oratus stay still, they should be able to snatch the last one in the group without the others knowing.

The other three agree to Sax's plan and, as the Rotam circle the opposite side of the section, the set takes up their positions. Sax gets the first opportunity, as it's his idea. The Stim's still going strong—the effect lasts for hours—and so when the Rotam go by, Sax has no trouble reaching out and grabbing one a couple of meters behind the others.

His claws dig into the creature's body and he lifts it off the track. It struggles, but from the side, the Rotam don't have much in the way of defense. He sees Bas give him a congratulatory tail twitch, and then they're turning to head to the gateway.

Which slides open. Before it should.

"The Oratus continue to live up to their reputation," the voice, hissing and deep, comes from what Sax hopes never to see. An Oratus, standing tall and clad in black, shining armor. The plates and helmet make him look ridiculous, and must be more limiting than a mask, but the Oratus doesn't seem to care. "Now, it's time for the Sevora to live up to ours."

Around him pour out Flaum, all aiming weapons at the set.

There's noise from the track too—the Rotam that just passed by have turned around.

Sax knows they're pinned. Trapped.

Dead.

The gates of Damantum stand tall in Ignos' evening light. Gilded gold and peppered with obsidian, which Malo says is intentional. An homage to Tutio. Charre signs decorate the sculpted columns. Some I recognize, and others I don't. It's a reminder that if I'm to preach to these people, I have a lot of learning to do.

As we near the city, the warriors break off. Malo dismisses them, and they disappear. Going to see their families, lovers, and friends.

Malo stays near me, along with Viera, who's trying to look everywhere at once.

"A city full of enemies," Viera says when I ask her why she's so tense. "Any Charre would love to put a knife in my back."

I can't disagree with that statement. Most Solare would want to do the same.

We make our way to the gates, pressing through the crowds of traders and merchants shifting in and out of the Charre capital, and two guards approach. Unlike Malo and his warriors, these do not wear any animal skins and are instead bare-chested, sporting leather skirts and sandals. Each of them hold spears, and wears a red feathered mantle. They look at me for a moment, apparently decide I'm no threat, and turn their attention to Viera.

If the Solare aren't worth attention, the Lunare get double.

"What have you brought us today, Malo?" the lead guard says.

"A priestess," Malo replies, pointing at me. "She'll go to Jakkan, and you'll see her soon. She hears Ignos, and says he wishes to give us miracles."

The warriors don't believe Malo's endorsement. They crack smiles, hide their laughter. I'm about to speak up when Malo continues, "This other one is Viera. A Lunare. Be careful of the weapon she holds, as it commands deadly power."

"Deadly power?" now the guards are interested. "We can't let her have it, then. Not if you mean to take her inside the city."

"You know the terms," Viera says this in Lunare tongue to Malo, and I translate when the guards stare and Malo looks to me.

"She says she won't give it up." I try to shrug, like it's just not going to happen, but I don't think they buy it.

"Unless you can make her?" Malo asks.

"I can't."

I don't want to try. There are certain things that I'm willing to risk for my friends, but disarming one of them in a place so obviously hostile? That seems like a bad idea.

Malo nods, apparently respecting my situation. Then he turns to Viera, who matches Malo's look with a defiant glare of her own. I don't catch it, but Malo darts forward, so fast, and grabs Viera's right arm. Keeps it away from the pistol.

The guards are almost as quick, and they have Viera restrained in moments. One of the guards untangles a rope from a loop on his skirt and ties Viera's wrists together.

Malo pulls the pistol, carefully, from Viera's holster. The Charre chieftain holds it in both hands, looking at it as though sight alone will reveal its secrets to him.

"Give that back." Viera struggles, but she's not making any headway.

"Tell her I'm sorry, but Viera can't be permitted to roam the city armed," Malo says to me.

"Stop fighting," I tell Viera. "You're only going to make it worse. They may just decide to kill you. How's that going to help?"

Viera looks for a moment like a rabid animal, caged and snarling, but as the ropes tighten the attitude fades. Her mouth soothes into a straight line. Her eyes are embers, and she directs their heat at Malo, who ignores it.

"If you're bringing them into the city, then she's your charge," the lead guard says. He holds forth the end of the rope to Malo, who takes it.

"I accept. She'll be taken care of and watched," Malo replies.

Then he turns to me, and motions me forward through those arched, yellow stone gates and into the city.

I want to argue. To say that Viera, now that she's unarmed, can be let free. Ignos stops me. Tells me that it's more important now to gain the trust of the city. Of these people. One Lunare isn't worth risking our dream.

Our dream. Not sure I ever wanted this, but now I'm too far in to back out, and I can't deny a growing part of me loves the adventure.

So I walk forward. Into the most bustling city I've ever seen. It's streets are packed with people shuffling back and forth. Many carrying baskets and bags loaded down with fruits and meats, cloth and clay urns. Stands are set up all along every corner and open space, connected right to the small houses behind them where the owners can wake up and start selling until they pass out at the end of the night.

The sounds of bargains being driven, coins being exchanged fill my ears, along with the smells of a thousand cooking scents and spices.

There's an undertone beneath it all that I pick up too. Of refuse and waste. Still, Damantum feels alive. As if the city is awake and has a spirit far more vigorous than my village ever did.

"This is my home," Malo says as he leads me through the streets. "It is everything to me, as it is everything to the Charre. What do you think of it?"

Do not insult it.

Like I need the reminder.

"It's overwhelming," I say. "I've never seen so much in one place before."

In truth, I notice, it is missing one thing: trees. There are so few. Damantum is all brown and sandy. Light-bleached and hot. What shade there is comes from the sharp corners of buildings, and not the leafy shadows of the jungle I love. So even as I take it in, I realize that Damantum is not, and maybe never will be, my home.

"You'll get used to it in time," Malo says. "Everyone does. The treasures that are here, the experiences, the people. It all is a lot, I know. Eventually you'll start to see why this is wonderful. You'll fall in love, like I have."

Viera stays silent during our walk. Every time I think to ask her a question, or even look at her, Ignos yells at me to stop. At first I argue, but then begin to think Ignos' advice is right; Viera's not the only captive I see in the streets. Many are led about in groups with ropes chaining between all of the them in a line. Nobody looks at them. Nobody acknowledges their bowed heads and scuffing bare feet.

Would a priestess?

No, Ignos says, and I agree. I won't be able to help Viera if I join her in the ropes.

We reach the Vaos. It is gigantic. Tall and monstrous and beautiful and horrendous at the same time. As I saw from the volcano, the whole temple is gilded in gold. It shines and shimmers at dusk, a flickering multitude. Halfway up the giant stone slabs that make up the Vaos' steps, there's a wide square door. One haloed by a set of four burning braziers.

"That's where you belong," Malo says to me. "Go in there, and you will meet our high priest, Jakkan. He will help you. He will teach you what you need to know so that you can give us what Ignos needs us to hear."

"Are you coming with me?" I ask.

"I'm not a priest, therefore I'm not allowed on the steps of the Vaos without permission."

I notice that Malo is right; despite the teeming masses of people moving through the courtyard around the great temple, many of whom stop to pray up to its altars, there are no bodies on the steps.

No one taking a careful walk up to the top. But at Malo's urging, I do.

I have to raise my knees high to get up, because the steps are not small. There are twenty of them to get to where the doorway begins.

Look at where you are. Already climbing above the mess. Keep moving, Kaishi, and we will make it.

When I reach the doorway, I turn to see if Malo and Viera are watching, but they're gone. Only crowds of people funneling by, a few casting curious glances up at me.

I'm alone.

There's only one way to go, though, so I look inside. It's a dark tunnel. Not a long one. Every meter, set into the stone walls, are small basins with candles flickering away.

I take hesitant steps.

The sound of the city dies as I go inside, and a cool breeze carries burning incense. The Vaos opens up to a central chamber, and I can see at least four doors off of either side. Standing in the middle, his back tight and frail, is a man. A design inked on his back, in various dyes so as to create a beautiful rainbow collage, is of Ignos at dawn, the golden orb and the multicolored bands of his blessings radiating out. As I watch, the man turns, unfolding his hands, which had been clasped for prayer, and grins at me. His right eye is milky white and there are gaps in his teeth, most of which are gold.

"Welcome," the man says, and his voice is strong and firm. Iron. "I've been waiting for you, Kaishi, supposed speaker for our god."

When Stim wears off, it's like coming out of a leap—everything speeds up and seems, at first, too real. Actions happen too fast. There's no time to think. Sax's body twitches in the room, one of the black ones, so that it seems like he's lying in the middle of blank space. The windows are closed, so there's really nothing other than Sax, the Sevora-stolen Oratus, and a quartet of watching Flaum.

"Yes, that must be painful for you," the Oratus says as it watches Sax breathe hard, heavy. "Stim, I take it?"

Three Flaum stand in the corners of the room, each one pointing a two-pawed miner at Sax. He's fairly sure that, if he had the Stim and a moment's surprise, Sax could move fast enough to take out at least two before the third vaporized him. That would still leave the Oratus, though, and that's the most important target.

"Can you speak at all, or is the prospect of me existing so terrible that you can't even form words?" the Oratus continues.

In a situation where sacrifice is not possible and attack is ill-advised, gather intelligence. Sax knows his training, so he lifts his head, ignores the pulsing headaches leftover from the Stim, and talks, "You are an abomination."

It's a strong opening, and Sax feels better for having said it. At least, until the Oratus laughs.

"Am I?" the Oratus replies, then considers for a moment. "Do you know what? I might agree with you. Look at me, in this armor? And look at you, in that mask, all pure."

Sax isn't sure what to say to this, so he stays quiet. Lets his eyes drift to the Flaum and checks their attention. Right now, they're still riveted. That's the Sevora control, though, not the Flaum themselves. Through the mask, Sax listens for the sounds of the others, but there's no pick-up. These buildings are thick, likely jammed with electronics. Their signal might not get through.

"You're probably wondering why we haven't shot you yet." The Oratus paces now, circling Sax like a predator, those talons clicking on the black floor. "It's a tricky thing, getting a working mask. We don't have a single one. All of the Sevora. Not one. Can you believe it?"

Sax can. The mask is a second skin. It'll only come off if Sax forces it to. Every other way would break it, and when the mask is broken, it takes care of its own elimination. Now Sax knows what the Oratus wants, and when you know what your prey desires, you can set a trap.

"Are you offering a deal?"

"Yes," the Oratus pauses, stares hard at Sax. "Take off the mask, and I'll let you live."

"You'll just give me to a Sevora. I'll be like you."

"Like me?" the Oratus resumes his circling. "You'll never be like me. You live once, while I live a thousand times, in many bodies. But you, this one life of yours, will last longer."

"I only need to tear you apart a single time." Sax opens his mouth wide, shows all of his teeth. They gleam in the low light, razor weapons waiting for their chance to strike.

Every child has nightmares. They see ghosts. Figments of stories that whirl in front of their eyes in the dead of night or, sometimes, when they're alone in the jungle in the middle of the day. The man in front of me comes from those nightmares.

His eyes, wrinkled and bordered with dark ink, stare at me. His face, etched in deep lines, appears to have seen a century, and holds all of the wisdom that went with it. His head is clear. Shaved. His body, in front of me, is thin and wrapped in a fine cloth that he pulls idly up over his left shoulder.

Here at last I see some evidence of Jakkan's position: his robe has many colors, and dyes are rare in both Solare and Charre. Reds and greens interspersed with dashes of blue. It makes me think of running by colorful trees. Yet, the idea strikes me as wrong. The painting isn't quite right, the streaks not where they should be. Not natural.

I get the idea that Jakkan rarely leaves the city. The jungle, if he's ever seen it, is a memory and not a core of his heart like mine.

"You see me," Jakkan says. "Tell me, what do I look like?"

Be careful. This one lays traps with his words.

I hear Ignos, but there's something in the way Jakkan speaks that compels me to answer. It might be the fact that he seems to be holding me as the center of his focus. As if I am the most important thing in his universe.

"You look nothing like the warriors that brought me here," I say.

I adopt, without realizing it, the language Father uses to speak with the elders. Respectful, honest. "Yet I don't think your strength comes from your arms and legs, but from your mind."

I'm about to go on, when Jakkan holds up a hand. Palm towards me. "My strength comes from Ignos," Jakkan says, and I hear a hint of reproach in his voice. "All strength does. What he chooses to grant us is what we have. You, as a priestess, should know this."

I'm not sure if this is a question or not, but Jakkan doesn't let me answer anyway. He turns away from me, walks over, in short easy steps, to a mottled black pot which seems to be boiling tea over hot coals. The small alcove bears the black-ash stains of many fires. All this leads me to believe Vaos is not only Jakkan's temple, but his home.

"Tell me your story," Jakkan says as he pours himself a cup.

My story is pretty simple. A young girl happens upon a god who crashed down from the sky. I can't tell Jakkan that. This is the Charre high priest. I have to come up with something better.

Ignos is ready for me. His words come streaming through my mind and I find myself spinning a tale I wouldn't have believed if I'd heard it myself.

"I began the same as you," I say, stating the words as Ignos presents them. "Chosen, not by any man, but by those greater. In the middle of a fast and crowded world, where disease, wildlife, or the spirit of your enemy could make for a swift end, I survived. I grew. I began to learn what it means to serve Ignos. This, for the Solare, means placing your tribe before yourself. Your people before your own life. It's simple, but important, and it's what keeps our village strong.

"However, my tribe did not let me hunt, because I am not a man. Impossible walls kept me out. So I did what I could and wished for more. I assisted in the rites, I learned to craft the clothes we wear, I practiced making the food that would feed my family. In time, Ignos recognized my devotion and my wish, which led me to you."

After I finish, Jakkan hands me some tea and I take a sip. Warm with a fruit-filled aftertaste. Pleasant, after a day of walking in the heat.

"Kaishi, if I am to let you stand in front of our glorious people and preach, I must make sure you do indeed hear the words of Ignos." Jakkan, sipping his tea between words, turns and vanishes into one of the side rooms.

I hear a clanking clatter of things moving around. I stay still. Finish my own tea.

"You will take this medal," Jakkan says as he comes back into the room, a stained bronze circle hanging from a thick ribbon around his hand. "You will wear it, then you will go to the Pits, on the west side of the city. You will be found there, and you will be shown to a juar, which you will tame in the name of Ignos. Should you succeed, they will give you a different medal, which you will bring back to me."

"Tame a juar?" the request is so strange that I don't understand it at first.

Jakkan nods again.

Ignos senses my sudden fear, but I don't have time for his questions right now. Jakkan's still talking, and if I'm going to get out of this, I have to listen to every word.

"You may think you are the first one to come to me," Jakkan continues. "The first one of our people, or any people, to come and demand to stand on this great temple and say they hear from Ignos. So I've devised a test. If you are truly favored, then Ignos will intervene. The task will prove as nothing to you, and you will be back here before long, ready to show us all how wrong we are."

If the Oratus is intimidated by Sax's display, he doesn't show it.

"This one said much the same." The Oratus taps the metal plate on his chest. "He made threats. Tried to hurt himself, to hurt me." He leans closer to Sax, who could swipe at him now, but that wouldn't guarantee the kill. So Sax feels hot breath on him and does nothing. "Do you know what happens when we take over your mind?

"You watch every moment. See out of your own eyes as you slaughter your friends. As you betray everything you are. This one is still here now. He is begging for you to leap at me and tear apart my throat."

Sax tires of listening. Tires of waiting for traps. Death comes for all Oratus at some time, and now it is his turn. So he bunches his legs and leaps. Sax knows he'll only have one strike, so he swings, in the air, and swipes right where the Oratus asked him to: at the vulnerable slit between the armor in the neck.

The Flaum don't fire. The Oratus doesn't flinch. Sax doesn't realize his mistake until he makes contact, his midclaws catching hold of the armor so his foreclaws can do the blood work. It feels like his every nerve comes ablaze with hot fire. The Oratus lifts Sax away, and Sax does nothing; all Sax can think, all he can do, is burn.

The Oratus throws Sax to the ground, and the mask, at least, blunts this force. It dulls the Oratus' kick a moment later too, sprawling Sax over onto his back. With a normal shock, Sax wouldn't be shaking now. Twisting and turning. The Oratus' armor seems to have melted away Sax's nerves. Left his body numb and unresponsive.

He watches the Oratus step over him. Sees the claws spread. There's a precise way to remove a mask, meant to be done only by the one wearing it. This Oratus knows what it is, no doubt he's ripped it from his captive's mind, and Sax is helpless as the creature leans down and pokes the claws on his four hands into Sax's palms. In the exact spots where, if Sax were to clench his own claws into his own hands, they would strike.

The mask peels away like a falling cloak; a brush of cool fabric along his skin, and it folds into a silvery pile at his feet.

"I didn't think that would actually work," the Oratus says as he bends over to pick up the mask. "A theory, stolen from this one's mind, and look at this. We have one, finally."

The Oratus runs a look at the Flaum in the room. "Carry him out, now. Let's take him before he gets his function back."

The three Flaum struggle to lift Sax and resort to dragging him across the metal floor, and then out into the open, down one of the pathways. Sax traces the lights on the ceiling. He knows exactly where they're taking him, and if he could snap his own neck, he would.

Some things are far worse than death.

23 / SHOPPING FOR SURVIVAL

The streets of Damantum flicker in the light of a thousand torches. Dancing shadows parade off of gold-glinted statues and homes as the city shifts into revelries. I walk down the front of the Vaos, playing with the medallion.

So these are giant, murderous creatures? Kaishi, I say we leave the city. Find a small village and grow our legend there. Then, when we have an army of the faithful equipped with my miracles, they'll all come groveling to your feet.

I reach the courtyard and look to the West. The roads leading that way dim, though the noises coming from that quarter ring over those coming from the rest of the city. Taming a juar. A jungle cat, though not many remain in Solare territory; hunted and driven away. I run my fingers along my mosswrap, cool and dry around my shoulders. It wouldn't do me any good against such a creature.

Exactly my point.

So instead of heading west, towards the Pits, I go straight. Walk by merchants pulling their carts in the opposite direction; heading home. More than a few people catch my eyes as I move, drawn to the moss, or my roving glances as I try to take in all I can of the city.

I feel their eyes on my face and its Solare features. When they notice the medallion, however, all of them look away and never turn back.

Jakkan's task is known throughout the city, apparently.

Yes, go towards the gates. Though I might suggest hiding that medallion, or throwing it in some dark alley. It's conspicuous.

I reach the main road, which, during the day, had been crowded with stands selling everything I could imagine. Now there are fewer, but the number still gives me a moment of panic. So many people, so many options. My hands find the medallion, hanging around my neck, and grip it tight. The firm metal calms my nerves. One foot after another. I slide between the crush of people, focusing on what I'm here for than the multitude of things around me.

What you're here for? Go to the gates. Your life is too valuable to waste!

I ignore Ignos. Push the god's voice to the back of my mind, so that Ignos' words come only as a buzzing, far off conversation. No Solare god would advocate fleeing such a challenge, so this must be another of Ignos' tests. My courage and conviction are being called into question, and for one of the first times in my life, I can control my own actions.

I will not run.

Ignos has no reply.

I find a stall covered in growing plants. Vines wrap the entire canopy, with wooden tables draped in urns overflowing with various leafy things. I go towards it, and barely begin to look them over before a short man appears, his long black hair tied on his head.

"I'm Zolin, and welcome to . . ." the shopkeeper trails off as he notices the medallion. Starts to turn away, but I put a hand on his shoulder.

"Please, why does everyone see this medallion and act strangely?"

"Because it's a sign of Jakkan's disfavor," Zolin replies. "You are stained by the high priest. Nobody would share in that."

"Stained? Jakkan gave me this medallion himself. As a sign I was on a mission from him."

"Then you're going to have a tough time of it." Zolin's still watching the medallion, like it's a snake that might bite him. "You won't find any help in Damantum wearing that."

"Fine," I reach to pull it off, but before I can even start, Zolin grabs the medallion and pulls it back down. Keeps it around my neck.

"No, you can't take it off! Not unless the high priest does it himself. Any guard sees you try to remove it, they'll kill you." As if thinking he could be implicated in the idea, Zolin shoots rapid looks around the crowd.

Nobody's paying us any attention.

"So I can't take it off or I die, but you're not going to help me if I'm wearing it?"

Zolin rubs his hands on his face. Looks hard at me. "You're young to get that prize. What'd you do to earn it?"

I tell the short version of my story. That I'd come to Damantum after a religious experience and that I want to become a priestess. Jakkan gave me the medallion and sent me on a quest to the Pits to tame a juar. When I finish, Zolin laughs.

"Tame a juar? That's a quick way to the grave," Zolin says.

"That's why I'm here." I point at the plants. "I need some curare. Do you have any?"

"What would you need that for? You're not a doctor." Zolin's left hand flies up to his tied hair, where it begins pulling on a loose strand and wrapping it around his fingers. "Unless you mean to . . ."

"I do," I say. "And bamboo. A small stick."

Zolin nods. "I've got those, but if you're planning what I'm thinking, you'll need to find something to do the dosing. I've not got that."

I see Zolin's eyes slip past me, across the avenue. "But you know somebody that does?"

"In this market? You can find anything." Zolin leads me around the stand, cutting a few leaves off of one particular plant and, using a mortar and pestle, crushing it into a thin liquid. "How'd you manage to learn about this beauty?"

"I'm not from around here," I answer. "We used it from time to time at home."

Zolin pours the liquid from the mortar into a small jar, caps it loose with a piece of wood. Then, from a rangy bamboo thicket at the back of the stand, where the reeds are nearly as tall as I am, Zolin cuts a section off. Using the same knife, Zolin cleans out the inside of the piece and then hands both things to me.

Then waits.

"I, uh, don't have anything to give you," I say when I realize what he's waiting for.

"Oh yes you do," Zolin says. "Here's what I'm asking. You make it past this, and I've got a feeling you're going to, you keep me in your prayers. And you come see me whenever Jakkan needs more incense, all right?"

I laugh.

"The needle?" I ask. "Where can I get that?"

Zolin points across the road to a stand that looks to be advertising hardier weapons. Jagged, curved swords and other big blades. At my hesitance, Zolin grunts, walks out from his stand and leads me across the street. Without letting me get a single word in, Zolin speaks to the surly blacksmith manning the shop and, in no time at all, comes out with a pair of sharp needles, each one a few centimeters long.

"Now you've got the materials, but do you have the skill?" Zolin asks.

"You'll know if you ever hear from me again."

"I hope I do, Kaishi," Zolin says. "There's grim rumors coming about the Lunare, and I'm thinking this city might need a new kind of priestess. One as smart as our warriors are deadly."

Without the mask, the seed ship's air is cool. There's a slight breeze—the recyclers keeping things fresh—and Sax smells the burn of disinfectant in the air. A hallmark on ships; the chemicals do their work to keep disease, deadly in compact confines, to a minimum.

It's this familiar scent, more than anything, that brings Sax down from a raging panic as the Flaum carry him out into the section. The sterile sting is a connection to things not quite so terrible as this moment, and the smell jolts his mind to what's important.

Namely, not becoming a Sevora toy.

The Flaum struggle to hold the Oratus' weight, and Sax sways through the air as the small creatures shift back and forth. As a result, Sax, whose numb muscles have his neck and head limp, gets a clear look at the captive Oratus following him. Sax's mask is in those claws, and the Oratus is snapping commands at seemingly nobody, which must mean that armor of his has a communicator in it.

Ideas for escape come and go, but they all have a common theme: Sax has to get his muscles moving again, or he's done.

It's a matter of trying. Like, after he's woken up in an awkward position, urging his legs to move. Flexing and loosening the muscles in his arms. At first, nothing happens, but gradually the feeling comes back. Twinging nerves burst like shocks.

Now the Oratus stops and watches as the Flaum maneuver Sax through a hard-railed fence gate. The ground here is smooth silver, spotless. Not scuffed with use like the rest of the section. As they move Sax around, he sees Bas, Gar, and Lan assembled in a line. There's a band of Flaum around them, holding rifles to the Oratus' backs. Captives all.

A new sound plays in the background. A burbling, shunting noise. Liquid current. Sax knows what they're doing now, and its confirmed when the Flaum swing him around to the side of a small pool full of purple-black ink. Not a birthing pool, but a hosting one.

Where the Sevora claim their victims.

Then, without fanfare, without a taunt, the Flaum throw Sax in. A fleeting moment in open space—the lower gravity hesitates before pulling Sax down—and then he hits the ink. The stuff pulls at him, sucking him inside and under the surface.

Before, in the birthing section, the Sevora were numerous. They gave off tremors as they swam towards him. Here, there's little indication. Sax guesses why when he feels the first tickles at the edge of his head. Only one in here. A Sevora that's earned its prized host.

The captured Oratus had said the armor and its electric shock was a test. One that had worked, for a while. One that, with the mask deflecting some of it, isn't able to keep Sax stunned long enough.

Time, and the relentless push of Sax's desperate anger, frees him from the shackles.

The Sevora tickles again. Trying to find a way inside Sax's mind. Unaware that it's no longer predator, but prey.

If the market had been bustling with commerce, the Pits hummed with death. I walk by the Vaos again to head towards Damantum's west side and leave behind the scent of incense for the harsh blow of burning flesh, of bloodstained air, and sweat's salty stink.

Yells echo down the alleys, punctuated with the roar of wild things. Crowds shift from those in traditional garb—the capes and loin cloths or skirts—to darker fare. Hair, on both men and women, begins to fall down around their shoulders instead of being held up in ties. Scars make their appearances. Grime is everywhere.

In the market people had met my eyes and looked away, here they don't notice I exist. All at once the buildings disappear and I'm pushing through a throng into a wide courtyard, cracked stones replacing the hard dirt beneath my feet. Crude wooden barriers divide the courtyard into four parts. Stakes nailed to others with bits of metal act as fences. Not enough by themselves to hold in a creature that wants to escape, but that's where the crowds come in; people ring each of the arenas, raising fists and passing coins. Others share skins full of what, I don't know.

I'll protest one last time. This is foolish. Needless. You're risking my miracles on a stupid chance.

I am, and I am not. I know I could turn around and walk out of the city. Perhaps even scrounge or find enough help to make it back to my village alive. But what then? Wait out the coming attack, either from the Charre or the Lunare? What end is that?

You could gather your strength, find a better way. One that includes fewer claws.

There isn't time. I'm here, now. I can do this. I can use, for once, what the jungle has taught me, what my people have given me. In my right hand, hidden beneath my cape, I hold the bamboo reed with the needle, soaked with Zolin's mixture, inside of it.

I'm ready.

Yet, nobody here seems to notice the medallion. Not a soul calls out to me, or tries to guide me through the press of people watching the fights. In one arena, a pair of what appear to be slaves fight each other with clubs, bashing away though neither looks like they want to.

The next pit over holds a strange event: several Charre warriors, wearing their bear skins, face off against a single captive. The warriors appear to be taking turns—darting in and exchanging blows with a desperate, bloody prisoner.

"This one is the last of his tribe," one of the watchers is saying as I go by. "He took down two bears himself. The bunch of them are fools for getting in there with the man, I think. Why risk death and waste a great sacrifice?"

On the other side of the courtyard sits a stack of bamboo cages with rope tying the stalks together. Foxes, small bears, and larger lizards pace, growl, and sleep inside. Other creatures I don't recognize. One is huge, with eight thick legs and covered in short white hair, and its large, eyeless head dips towards me as it laps up some foul-smelling slop from a shallow bowl on the ground.

The juar waits at the end. Lazing on a mat, with a leg of some animal set before it. Dinner. Which is a good sign. The predator might not be hungry when I step into the ring with it.

I move closer to the cage. Look harder at the animal. Its tanned fur seems healthy, and when the juar yawns, I see its jagged teeth, sticking out from its mouth at all angles, are long and sharp. We consider juar to be shredders, to be uncaring predators who will slash and snap at anything that moves. Or even things that do not—I've seen a coconut bearing the scars of a juar's rage.

Not every animal earns a caring treatment here, but the juar appears to be a lucky one. I come close, my face near the bars, and the big creature, standing taller than me, stares back with amber eyes. Slowly, I draw up my right hand.

"What are you doing? Getting a look at the competition?" a brash voice sounds right behind my ear and a thick arm claps down on my left shoulder. "Don't you worry, you'll get your chance soon enough."

I look and see a large, round man whose withering teeth and clawed face leer at me. "Been a while since Jakkan sent another one to the Pits. I thought for sure all the upstarts had realized pushing the head priest was a quick way to die."

"He gave me this." I, with my left hand, hold up the medallion.

The big man doesn't bother looking at it.

"I know who you are. Word's been spreading all night. You're the one that says she can talk to Ignos, right?"

"I can."

"Better get chatting, then, cause you'll be needing some help once those warriors get done with that poor soul over there. Soon as he's down, you're in." Then the round man turns, bellows something over the clamor of the crowd, and heads away.

I wheel back towards the juar cage. Bring the bamboo reed up to my mouth with my right hand while cupping my left in front of my face, as if to quiet a cough. I take a deep breath, and blow hard into the reed. I don't see the needle fly, but then, I don't need to. The juar yelps, hisses, and bats at its chest.

Not where I want the shot to hit. The neck would have been far better. The chest takes time to circulate. Too much time, going by the size of those paws.

Behind me, the crowd bursts into a frenzy of yelling and shouting. I catch enough words to know the cause. The bear warriors have finished their business. The captive is dead.

My turn.

The tickling becomes full on contact as the Sevora finds its target: Sax's aural cavities. Slight pricks of pain as the Sevora digs its barbed tentacles into Sax, and the moment's now. If Sax is going to survive, he has to act.

But slow.

There can't be any hint to those above the surface that something is going wrong. His left foreclaw moves, sluicing through the thick ink up towards his own head. The Sevora slips in—Sax can feel its body contorting, pressing against the inside of him. The barbed tentacles start to retract.

Too late.

Sax dips a claw into his own head, and when it makes contact with the Sevora, the parasite freezes. Sax does not. He pushes harder, feels the claw break the Sevora's skin, and pulls back. An explosion goes off in Sax's mind as the Sevora realizes what's happening and tries to fight. Tries to squirm inside Sax's brain. Its tiny tentacles are no match, however, for an Oratus arm, and Sax's claw is hooked enough to keep the wriggling Sevora on it until the parasite is out.

Without pausing, Sax pulls his claw down, turns his head, and shoves the Sevora in his mouth. Ink floods in too, but its designed to keep the parasites alive and tastes like nutrient soup. Good for washing down Sevora squid.

Sax doesn't even need to breathe in here—the ink carries with it the oxygen he needs to survive, so Sax waits a few moments. Figures it would take a bit of time for a Sevora to get control of its new host, learn how the muscles work. Sax does a silent count to a hundred.

Then curls his legs beneath him and pushes against the pool's floor. Surfaces slowly. With extreme control. How a Sevora would do it, hopefully.

The ink drips away from Sax and he's able to see everyone's stares, even the Flaum who ought to be paying close attention to the three deadly Oratus right next to them.

They're waiting to see what's come out of the pool. Sax dashes his eyes around, holds contact with Bas for just a moment so that she knows, and then he wades to land. Walks to the captive Oratus, who tilts his head in a nod towards Sax.

"Give yourself time," the captured Oratus says. "These bodies have many limbs. No need to rush." He turns to the other three Oratus. "You see what's become of your leader? The same thing that will become of you. Give us your masks, save yourself some pain, and join us."

"What is your name, friend?" Sax hisses. In a moment, his claws will be ripping apart that armor. Tearing off the head inside of it. Sax wants to know who he's about to end.

"Avan," the Oratus replies, and Sax can hear the question in his voice. "However, shouldn't you know that already?"

Sax replies with something other than words: his mid-claws stab forward, biting into Avan's hard armor, while his foreclaws swipe at Avan's head. A normal, trained Oratus would have seen the attack coming. Would have reacted in time.

Avan is not a trained Oratus. Avan's reaction is to jerk back. Or try to.

Sax tears at the helmet, rending its straps to pieces and ripping it off of Avan's head. He knows there's a chance Avan could trigger the electric shock again, send Sax into a numbed fit, so he's got to move fast.

Then he's not holding Avan anymore. Just an armor plate. Avan's backpedaling, a spiderweb of clasps dangling from his chest. Which is when Sax understands why Avan didn't try to shock him again: the mask. Avan still holds it in his claws.

The shocking armor didn't destroy the mask while Sax had it deployed, but a dormant mask is like cloth—easy to tear apart. As Sax tosses aside the armor—it's lightweight here in space—he catches hints of the battle apart from him. Skittering panic from the Flaum as they try to organize some sort of defense. Hissing anger from the other three Oratus as they rend that defense to pieces.

Surprise is the great equalizer, and Sax has it here.

That advantage dies with every second, though. Avan's already pulling for his miners, and Sax can't give him any more time. Without a mask, Sax is vulnerable, so he takes to the air. Leaps forward, all four claws extended and sharp.

Avan ducks away to his right, barreling through a fence to a sparse target range. Behind him loom the four core buildings of the section. Sax catches the ground, digs in those claws and bursts after Avan.

Part of Sax wonders where the other Sevora are? Four armed Oratus and all this giant seed ship sends are a few Flaum? He expected battalions. Artillery. Real resistance.

It comes a moment later. Sax is bounding after Avan, his claws outstretched, shining, when the section's lights extinguish, plunging everything into darkness.

The caretaker, the man who'd grabbed me by the juar cage, takes me by my shoulders and guides me through a parting crowd to the fighting pit. Inside the wooden fencing, the gray stones are splattered with blood, spit, and spoiled food lobbed in from outside. The caretaker leads me inside the stakes, then looks at me.

"Tell me, priestess, have you ever fought a juar before?" the caretaker says, his voice saying that he already knows the answer.

I stare back at him, figuring I can use any hints he deigns to give me, and shake my head.

"It's not so hard as it looks. Nobody expects you to kill the thing, even Jakkan. The point is to live long enough. You do that, and you'll prove yourself worthy of the high priest's attention."

"How long?"

"Ah, see, that's the trick," the caretaker points across my pit to the next one. The one that had contained a pair of slaves. It too appears empty. "In another minute, someone will be entering that pit. Same as you did now. They'll be facing another juar. All you've got to do is outlast them. See?"

"Outlast them?"

"Juars need to eat, priestess. They like their food fresh. You want yours to go hungry." The man laughs as he walks out of the arena.

This is a savage game. Look for a way to run, Kaishi. It does us no good to stay.

Except there isn't anywhere to go. People crowd up to the fences, their faces wild and leering, full of drink and tossing coin back and forth. Taunts and jeers mingle with the odd shout of encouragement.

I try to close off from the frenzy. Fall into myself. I must be able to think if I'm going to get out of here alive.

The posts on the north side appear the weakest, and the crowd there is thinnest at the main passage. When you run, I would go that way.

Cheers rise up, coupled with an animal's harsh snarls. No, a pair of them. Now the crowds move quick, if only to get out of the way. I see the juar I'd shot in the cage, hissing at the end of a rope collar as the caretaker pulls it along. The rest of the leash leads away from the collar to the thick coil around the man's arm. The caretaker has slipped on a thick coat of leather that covers his chest, arms, and neck. Gloves woven in with gray metal wrap around his hands.

Protection I don't have.

A shout rings out behind me. My competition. In the other pit, pushed out into the open, wearing only a tattered robe and nothing else, stands Viera. She's whirling at the crowd, her neck and face red from yelling. Not that she can understand the Charre, or they her.

When Viera finishes her look around, she catches sight of me and stops.

"What're you doing here?" Viera calls across the pits.

"A test. Same as you," I reply.

Behind me, the caretaker leads the juar up to the side of the pit. The creature lopes over the low barrier into the arena with lazy familiarity, though its collar keeps the beast tight to the caretaker. I retreat to the far end of the pit as the caretaker slips the juar's collar over a thick post, tying the juar at a distance.

"This isn't a test," Viera yells back. "It's an execution."

"Only for one of us." I watch the juar as it watches me. I see, thankfully, my dart is already having an effect. While the creature prowls back and forth, its eyes look heavy and its breathing heaves.

Sleep will come soon.

"What do you mean?" Viera sounds frustrated. "I can't understand a damn thing they're saying."

"If you die, I live," I shout back. "Or the other way around."

A second set of growls comes out from the other side of the Pits as the caretaker leads a second, mangier, juar towards Viera's arena. This one's coat holds more gray, and it's gaunt. Decaying with age. But the creature lets none of its years show in its eyes, in its sharp claws that slash at any poor reveler that comes too close.

"It's insanity," Viera cries. "How can they do this?"

I have no answer. No demand from Ignos calls for pitting the unarmed against wild creatures. This is simple bloodsport. Pleasure at pain.

The caretaker leads Viera's juar to the corner of his pit, the closest one to mine, and then takes up the second juar's leash. Holding one leash in each hand, the man lifts the coils high and begins a sort of song. The crowd joins in, and while I can't catch all of the words, it sounds like a prayer. A blessing for the fight.

As they sing, I stare at the juar, at its big green eyes. My death lies in those pupils.

The song ends, but before the last note dies away, the caretaker lets the ropes fall free, gives the juars all the slack they need to get around the pits.

"How do I fight one of these things?" I hear Viera yell.

"Keep moving!" I reply.

I sidestep to the opposite corner of the pit, keeping my eyes on the juar across from me, who watches my shifting without comment.

Technically, nothing is keeping the juar in the ring. It could leap the barrier and tear into the yelling crowd, but it doesn't. Afraid, maybe, of the rope tying it to the caretaker. What the caretaker could do to it.

Watch out!

I jerk my eyes back and see the juar bounding towards me. The great beast takes one lope, then bursts into a leap at my throat. I do what I'd done in the jungle in games with other children: I roll. Fall on the stones and twist. I hear the juar strike the rock behind me. Claws tug on my moss wrap; the dried vines tearing apart. I don't pay attention to that, only to pushing off of the ground and running away.

Back along the juar's rope, towards the corner and the grinning caretaker beyond those wooden stakes.

Behind me, the juar tries a roar that starts strong and fizzles to a yawn. The crowd laughs, and one man calls out to the caretaker and asks if the juars had their rest.

"Plenty of it!" the caretaker replies. "They sleep all day as it is. This one's just got to wake up!"

The caretaker snaps his rope, and I see the crack wind to my juar and jerk its collar, stopping its yawn. The juar snarls back at the caretaker, then its eyes move to me. Slow, though. Not much longer and the creature would collapse. Behind me, the crowd around Viera's pit begins clapping and shouting. I want to look, want to see if the Lunare has fallen, but I don't dare glance away from my own monster.

The juar lunges towards me, ready to pounce again, and I tense. Ignos is screaming in my head to run, and I try to ignore the god's panic. No time for that now. The juar opens its mouth wide, long fangs sharp and white. Tilts its head slightly, locking on my face. Ready to lunge for my neck.

Ready to go for the kill.

I feel the stiff wood boards of the pit's border against my back.

Nowhere left to retreat. The caretaker, directly behind me, is laughing. The crowd hushes. They know the moment is coming, just as I do.

Those claws will be finding their mark.

The first thing Sax does when his vision goes black is drop to the ground. Lower his profile. What is dark for him will not be for others; Bas, Gar, and Lan still have their masks on and those will flip to show the infrared spectrum: greens and reds playing off of heat signature. The Sevora may have something similar.

Sax does not. His only immediate comfort is that Avan, without a helmet or mask of his own, is probably seeing the world as the same endless black as Sax is.

"This way!" Bas' voice rasps out from the nothing, and Sax traces the sound behind him.

Claws scratching against metal floors mingle with other noises—the moaning of injured Flaum, the clatter of larger things running through the section. The Sevora wouldn't have made this move unless they had a plan.

The Oratus must make their own quickly.

Bas meets Sax out of nowhere. She taps him on the shoulders with her tail, which Sax then grabs. She leads him along the path, and Sax has enough memory of the section to know where they're going.

If they can't tell where their opponent might be, they need to find ways to limit the options.

"The door is shut," Lan's voice this time. A higher hiss than Bas. "The control panel isn't responding."

There's a bang, followed by a second and a slight tremor as something hits the ground.

"That works too," Lan sighs.

There's a deep laugh that Sax attributes to Gar, and then Bas is moving again. Sax follows her, reading the movements in her muscles to duck beneath the door's threshold. He recognizes the feel of the place, the sudden absence of moving air, and the deadening of noise from outside.

They're back in one of the buildings. Ready to hole up.

"He took my mask," Sax states the obvious, reminding the other three that he's blind and unarmed.

"How?" Bas asks and Sax relays the details.

"Then they'll want the rest of us," Lan says after it's done. "Protocol says we destroy them. And ourselves."

"We're not at that stage yet," Sax replies.

The outcome isn't certain. Yes, they're likely trapped in a section with a seed ship's worth of Sevora getting ready to make an attack, but Oratus don't give in to despair.

"I won't be a plaything for some parasite," Gar says.

"Then don't be," Bas hisses. "The Sevora know our protocols as well as we do. They'll be expecting us to hole up, to guarantee that none of us are taken. So we do something else."

"We attack." Sax agrees with his pair. "Split apart. They'll need to restore some power to open the gateway, and when it does, rush it. Move quickly and focus on getting through, not killing them."

"What are we waiting for, then?" Gar asks, and they all agree.

No point in waiting for the Sevora to come after them. The Oratus are predators. Everything on this ship is prey.

The juar hesitates. I wait, but it doesn't jump. Instead, the juar opens its mouth wide and its tongue lolls off to the side. Relief runs through me like ice—the poison is taking effect.

The crowd laughs, and the caretaker shouts at the juar, cracking the rope again. I sneak a glance Viera's way, but people have filled in the space between us. I can't see her.

Pay attention!

I snap back to see the caretaker's managed to get the juar moving. Instead of looking at me, though, the creature snarls towards its master. It crouches, those big legs tensing, and leaps towards me.

Over me.

It blocks out the lights as its mass of fur and claws dives above my head.

The juar clears the wooden stakes and flies into the caretaker. The beast knocks him over, clawing at openings in the man's armor. Biting at his face, trying to get through. The caretaker fights back, wrestling to throw the juar off, but the beast is too big, too agile, too angry.

You can either watch the man get eaten, or you can run, Kaishi. You know which one I'd choose.

Ignos makes a good point. I clamber over the barrier, unmolested since the crowd is too distracted to notice me, and finally get a look at Viera's arena. The Lunare is sporting some deep scratches. Bleeding, but she's still standing. Her juar isn't even watching Viera anymore, but is staring, open-mouthed, at the caretaker's scuffle.

The crowd, meanwhile, begins to back away. Realizing, maybe, the juar may win the fight and come for them next. Some flat out run; dashing from the courtyard into the city streets. Some call for guards.

With a growl, the second juar follows its rope and joins its brother. Its teeth and claws sink into the caretaker's leather, tearing it to pieces.

"Come on, priestess," Viera shouts as she climbs over the barrier towards me. "I say we leave before anyone knows we're still alive."

The courtyard breaks into full pandemonium. Guards, holding weighted nets, run by us towards the juars. Caretakers of other pits join them. The rest of the crowd alternates between fleeing and calling for new bets, now that the stakes have changed. I'm splattered with someone's drink as I push through the Charre, and I see more fun than fear in these faces.

From one show to the next.

So when Viera's hand pulls me through the last of the mess, I'm relieved. We're out of the courtyard and back into the dark streets. At the first deserted alley, though, Viera stumbles aside. She leans against a house wall, away from the bustle. Torchlight sneaks in from the street, but most of what I see is shadow. Shapes in the stone reveal, upon a closer look, tracings of Charre animal gods.

"You need something for those wounds," I say, looking at Viera's body. Several deep cuts on her chest and arms bleed freely; long gashes with white puckering at the edges.

"Thanks for letting me know," Viera replies, but her voice is taut. "You don't happen to know where a doctor is in this city? Anyone that won't turn me in on sight?"

I shake my head. "I don't have any friends here. These are not my people."

Viera sinks against the wall until she's sitting in the dirt. "Isn't that just fantastic? Your people. I thought the whole point of you coming was to make these your people?"

"I'm supposed to tell them about Ignos," I say. "Then, if they believe what I say, they might help me."

"Any chance that belief is coming soon, and with medicine?"

What would Jakkan say if I went back to the temple with Viera?

What would the high priest do?

Viera groans. Jerks my thoughts back to her. Someone who protected me. Helped me.

I can't leave her here to die.

"Come on. I don't know a doctor, but I do know someone who may help." I offer my hand, and this time it's me lifting Viera to her feet.

I sling her arm over my shoulders. Together, we walk through the streets. Curious glances from the few Charre running the around this late, the imperious stares from guards on their way to the Pits. Most don't bother with a second look, and those that do see my medallion and quickly turn the other way. For once, I like being the outcast.

Unwanted and dangerous.

The Vaos towers above the surrounding houses and blazes with torches set on every step. A shimmering, fiery pathway to the home of the Charre's chief priest. An appropriate image, I suppose, for Jakkan.

Both of us climb, slowly, towards Jakkan's chambers. I don't know what I expect, but seeing Jakkan standing with a pair of other men wearing priestly ropes doesn't surprise me. The small boy in the middle of the room does.

Jakkan recites some sort of chant while the other two priests, using colored paste, paint the child in intricate designs. When we, with Viera leaving a bloody trail, walk into the room, all of them look at us, but none of them stop.

Jakkan, without breaking his recitation, catches my eyes and nods towards his water basin. There's a cloth there. I lead Viera around the ceremony, keeping as quiet as I can, and begin to wash the Lunare. Viera, for her part, sits on the floor and closes her eyes. Her breath rasps in and out. With torches flickering and a solemn prayer droning in the background, I focus on wiping the cloth back and forth, gently cleaning away the blood from her wounds, washing out the dirt and grime.

These are vicious cuts. If we were back among my friends, they could be healed in moments. As it is, you'll need to resort to stitching. Or cruder methods.

I look around, but there doesn't appear to be any needle and thread. No way to perform the stitching. Viera's cuts continue to bleed. If there's no way to stitch, to close the wounds, then what?

Fire, Kaishi. She'll hurt, but she'll live. At least for now.

There are plenty of metal instruments in the room. Ceremonial brands, irons. I take one, lift it softly as the priests continue coating the boy in swirling art. Patterns I recognize as the Charre Emperor's sigil. A helmet and a rolled scroll combining with the glowing orb of Ignos. The crest of the Emperor.

Who is this child? What is his purpose?

I'll ask those questions later.

I hold the brand in the torch flame, keep it there till the metal begins to glow a warm orange. Then, lifting it out carefully, I angle it towards Viera.

"I'm sorry. This will hurt." I whisper the words, though Viera looks like she's unconscious.

I press the brand close. Nearly brushing the angry red wound.

A light touch. Brief and then on to the next spot. We're trying to seal the blood, not cook her.

I go to work. Press the brand to the open flesh. It sizzles, smokes, burns and turns white-pink in front of me. Scarring and sealing.

Viera's eyes shoot open, and she might have screamed except I shove the balled up, bloody cloth between Viera's teeth. Keep it there as I guide the brand along Viera's gashes. Scar them white. Stop the bleeding.

Keep the Lunare alive.

Without saying so, the four of them separate into their pairs. Gar and Lan leave first, angling to the left. Bas and Sax will go right, and then both sets will turn towards the gateway, approaching it from opposite angles. The unspoken side of this is that whichever pair draws the Sevora will sacrifice themselves, leaving the remaining two to complete the mission.

It is grim. It is required.

Sax feels no sadness as they leave the building, only urgency. Determination. A desire to find Avan and destroy the taken Oratus.

Sax holds on to Bas's tail with his foreclaws, though she provides him with a Flaum miner. Their own weapons are missing—taken after their capture and not present at the birthing pool. Flaum miners are too small for Oratus claws, so Sax holds it with both midclaws. Awkwardly.

Back outside the building, the groans of the wounded have stopped. It's quiet, except for the clatter of Oratus claws on the surface. The sheer silence unnerves Sax. It's not in an Oratus to be quiet. They are destructive, not made for stealth.

"Do you remember our Enlightenment?" Sax whispers to Bas, a

noise that sounds the same as air leaking from a pressure pipe—high pitched and static-y.

"How could I forget a dying star?"

The flares had been beautiful, a gift after the trials of their pairing. The two of them had watched from the radiation-shielded deck of the station called Nova, designed and used exclusively for viewing interstellar phenomena. Nova would stay at this particular star until a solar storm destroyed it. Then a new Nova would be built wherever was deemed most beautiful.

Wherever would convince new Oratus that the galaxy was a place worth saving.

Oratus had three moments in their lives when frivolous things were permitted: the death of a pair, the Enlightenment, and Restoration—if an Oratus reached an age or suffered an injury that required severe medical attention. Sax has experienced only one of these, and the short time with Bas and an exploding star dominates his memories when he isn't fighting for his life.

Sax is fine with that, though. He doesn't want his senses to dull. His claws to lose their sharpness or his teeth to forget their taste for the flesh of his enemies.

But what brings him back to the Enlightenment now is the darkness. "Do you remember," Sax says. "How they closed the shield for a minute? How the whole room went dark and the only thing you could hear was your own breathing?"

"Your vents the loudest of all."

"I was excited." Sax grips tighter as Bas lurches up and over another fence.

"I felt it. You. Your heartbeats through your claws. It was the first time I understood what it meant to be a pair."

"A feeling that has never left me." Sax would say more, except in front of them, up steps that Sax can't see, an arch of green lights springs to life. The gateway. And, haloed in front of it, Avan.

By the time I'm done burning Viera's wounds, the ceremony behind me is over. Jakkan falls silent, and the two priests escort the painted boy from the chamber. Viera, after gnawing through most of the cloth in her mouth, simply passes out and lets me finish the cauterizing.

When I lift the brand away from the last cut, from the gray puckering flesh that, at least, no longer seeps blood onto the floor, I too feel like collapsing.

Nicely done. I'd even let you cauterize me. If I had a body.

Using fire to heal. I've seen it done before, though I'd never been a part of it myself. A desperate measure for only the most serious wounds. If there had been a poultice. If there had been needles, then perhaps I could have stitched her up. Bandaged the wounds and left Viera without that burn. But I don't know this city, and Jakkan offered no assistance.

"I see you have failed," Jakkan says when I set the brand down. "I see you return to me with the same medallion you wore when you left."

"I did not fail," I reply, not taking my eyes away from Viera. "I survived the Pits. As you asked."

"I did not ask you to survive. I asked you to return with a different medallion. You have not done so, and therefore you have failed."

Jakkan's words are too much. After surviving the juar. After dragging Viera bleeding through the streets of a city I do not know, where people stare at me as if I am the enemy. As if I am not to be touched. Being told I had failed falls on me like a searing weight, and I push back.

I grab the brand with my right hand and whirl towards Jakkan, stabbing it towards his face.

"You can say what you like. I lived. I survived your trap." I take a step forward, and Jakkan stays where he is. The brand comes close to the priest's face, but he does not waver.

"Tell me," Jakkan says. "Did you accomplish what I asked?"

The brand feels good in my hand. Strong. Heat still radiating from the front of it. With a short jab, I could shove it right into Jakkan's eye. Or perhaps swing it at his neck. The priest looks unarmed. Vulnerable.

What then?

Ignos unleashes a cascade of thoughts: What would come after such a strike? The people of the city would not love me for killing the high priest. How could I say Ignos wants this to happen? Wants the Jakkan murdered in his own sacred temple?

"No, I did not," I say the words, but keep the brand up. My eyes strong. Not my fault I failed an impossible task.

"Then you learned something. Do not let your emotions, do not let the moment carry you away from the facts at hand. A priestess must always, if she is to lead the people, be able to know what is right, no matter her surroundings." Jakkan looks past me to Viera on the ground. "Who is this woman?"

"She fought in the Pits with me. We survived," I launch into a quick version of the story that Jakkan hears without emotion.

Without reaction.

"You have led her here. Dripped her blood on my floor. Burned her wounds with a sacred instrument," Jakkan grasps the brand I hold, his hand touching mine on the cool end of the metal. "Do you understand the sacrilege that you have committed? To save a nonbeliever?"

"I made a vow to protect her, and she did the same for me," I say. "Ignos would understand."

Jakkan rips the brand out of my hand. Tosses it across the room, where it hits off of the wall to the ground. Gives Viera a dismissive look. "She will be fine for now. Come with me."

We sweep out of the chambers, towards the steps. I spare one last glance at Viera, who's still unconscious. Then I follow Jakkan all the way up to the top of the Vaos. He stops and rests one hand on the East altar. Waits for me to take everything in.

The view is incredible. Unlike anything I've ever seen before. The blazing of a hundred thousand torches lights up the streets like a glittering ocean in the dark. Above me, the stars fade against the orange firelight, as if Damantum exists in a world of its own, banishing the outside with the glow of its people.

"I always find Damantum more beautiful at night," Jakkan says. "When you have proof of all the life that is here. A Charre lit each of these fires. A Charre interested in preserving our city. Our livelihood, our civilization. So long as these torches are lit, Damantum will continue. Ignos will be worshipped."

"Why did you bring me here?" I say.

"I've inquired about you," Jakkan replies. "From Malo, from the warriors that journeyed with you. They all believe what you claim. To a man. They say you hear from Ignos himself. They say that you will take my place."

At this last, Jakkan looks straight at me. I expect an accusation, hatred or jealousy to show. Jakkan, however, keeps the same blank slate. He gives no hints to me as to what he wants, as to what he needs me to say.

All of my life, I'd been given little hope of power. Little chance of position. My destiny had been chosen by my sex. Standing on top of the Vaos, for once, I cannot tell where my own future lies. Options abound. So many paths to follow. And all of them could be swept away if Jakkan chooses to cast me down.

"I don't want your place," I say. "Ignos chose to bring me here. I'm only following his will."

"And his will must be respected." Jakkan nods at the medallion around my neck. "This first task proves that Malo was right. Ignos favors you. How many escape the Pits when faced with the juar?"

I don't know. Jakkan doesn't wait for me to answer.

"None," Jakkan says. "None."

"They said the one who lives longer gets to leave?"

"A ploy to get some fight from you." Jakkan almost looks sad, but then his face slides into the straight mask. "Should your friend have fallen, the crowd would have cheered your own death moments later."

"How was I supposed to survive, then?"

"You found a way." Jakkan says, as if that answers the question, then waves away my open mouth. "You understand my responsibility. The Emperor looks to me for Ignos' guidance. Therefore I must be sure that any who claims to speak for him truly hears his words."

"I escaped the Pits, as you said. Isn't that enough?"

"You may have his luck, but are you truly his vessel? Tomorrow there will be a sacrifice. For the boy that you saw, in honor of his approaching manhood. In honor of his parent's life. You will perform it. You will conduct the ritual, and you will give us a message from Ignos. Do it well, and I will grant you your audience with the Emperor. More so, I will grant you a chance to join me. To lead the city into the light it deserves."

When the two of us descend, some hours later, after conversations of home and life in the city, Jakkan goes first. I follow, almost bumping into the high priest when he stops at the entrance to the chambers. Jakkan turns to me, a small smile on his face. "It seems the one you rescued has no wish to thank you."

I look around Jakkan and see only dried blood stains on the temple floor. Viera is gone.

Sax only has a moment to think before the gateway opens. In that moment, hope and hunger mix with the sudden light to push him forward. He bounds past Bas, clenches his legs, and leaps towards Avan's shadow.

The low gravity gives Sax plenty of lift, and he drops the miner as he glides through the air. He has no chance of hitting anything with it anyway, and the satisfaction of a laser is nothing compared to the visceral cutting of his claws.

The gateway doesn't wait for Sax. It shunts open, sliding up into the wall of the seed ship, and reveals a waiting Sevora force. More Flaum, because the standard-issue troops are always there, but what catches Sax's attention as he flies are the Slivers; worm-like things with gossamer wings that glow violet as they fly over Avan's head.

Each of the four Slivers has, grafted onto their many legs, heat stingers: small lasers that, individually, are nothing more than annoying. Together, the simultaneous blasts can overwhelm a target's nervous system. Send them twitching to the floor. Means the Sevora aren't giving up on capturing the Oratus after all.

The Slivers, though, didn't expect to see Sax flying through the air towards them, claws extended and ready to rend. He hits a Sliver before it has a chance to move, and Sax doesn't even have to bite—his weight alone crumples the fragile creature and they both plummet towards the gateway floor.

Avan, and his new Flaum friends, notice. And, as Sax crashes down into their mix, they scatter. Sax doesn't even get a swipe in at Avan before the captive Oratus is gone. Pressing through the Flaum and through the gateway.

Coward.

Sax would follow, but he's otherwise occupied. The Flaum are overcoming their own surprise, turning their miners on Sax. Sitting still means a quick roasting at the hands of their lasers, so Sax moves.

Surrounding an Oratus at close range is like being in a razor blade tornado: Sax darts at a Flaum near the gateway, while his tail whips towards the Flaum left of that one. He digs his claws into fur, then leaps off to another one. Red bolts flash where he was, coupling with the green light of the gate and the filtering blue aura of the new section beyond to create a washed out strobe effect.

Sax barely registers the faces. The targets. Without the Stim, he can't keep up with his own instinct, and simply responds to touch. To the tear of claw through cloth. To the thwack of his tail swatting another Flaum to the ground. It's a massacre, a chaotic frenzy.

Until sudden burning drives Sax down.

Dust motes dance in the light of dawn as I open my eyes and look out through the archway from my room. One of four leading off of Jakkan's main chamber in the Vaos, the high priest had let me settle into the spare space. The mat on the stone floor suffices, though I prefer soft jungle ground where I don't wake with aches in my back.

Not that it had been a restful night anyway: Jakkan didn't spend any time worrying about Viera, but instead showed me the scrolls with depictions of Charre rites, told me to read, and then vanished into his own chambers.

I'd taken the scrolls and sat next to the fire. Read one after another. Familiarized myself with tales and odes, songs and prayers, some of which were known to me and others far different. The Charre rites are like relatives—their shapes and duties recognizable, their names changed. So similar that I started putting in Solare words where they didn't belong. Found myself sinking into the stories told around my village's campfires instead of the ritual tales in front of me.

I suggest you find a way to your bed, Kaishi. You're turning the scroll awfully slow, and as much as I like rereading the same words endlessly, it's become a bit boring.

But I had to learn. I shook my head. Tried to open my eyes all the way.

Not all of it, and not right now. I've read everything you have, and I'll feed it to you during the ceremony. However, I can't lift your arms. Can't speak from your mouth. So if you don't have the energy to manage that, then we're both going out the grisly way.

I supposed that if I was going to trust anyone to get a ceremony right, it would be a god. So I accepted Ignos' offer and stumbled to my chamber, collapsed on the mat and sank into a too-short slumber till, what seemed like moments later, Jakkan woke me with the breaking of dawn.

The high priest holds a new, beautiful cape for me. Weavers have speckled the cloth in oranges and blues. Expensive dyes. Colors only worn by those of noble rank, or that had given their lives to Ignos.

Jakkan himself says so, and he wears similar finery. Gold hoops hang from his ears and another ring from his nose. His hair is tied in a knot on top of his head with silver bands. His hands hold still more jewelry, which he hands out to me.

"Today these are yours," Jakkan says. "If this goes as you wish it, then tomorrow you shall have your own."

The earrings, speckled with rubies and sapphires, appear to be small depictions of Ignos. I slip them on, then comes the piece for my nose. A swooping golden band made to look like waves of light in early morning. Thus adorned, I wait for Jakkan, who had retreated to his chambers. This time he emerges with a couple of pots. Each one filled with dye. He sets them down in the middle of the room and then, nodding to me, goes to the far window.

This side of the Vaos looks out to the West, opposite where Ignos rises. On the mountains overlooking the city, I can see Ignos' dawn display: purple, brown, orange and yellow as the light glances off the peaks and the slopes below to paint the fields in Ignos' colors.

"It is the most divine part of the day," Jakkan says. "Evidence that Ignos' will is truly beautiful. We must remind the people of that. Today you have a chance to do so. I will be there, yet you alone will speak the prayers. I trust you have learned what you wish to say?"

I nod, though in truth, I only have glimmers. Before, at the crashed ship and at my village, I had spoken from my heart. From Ignos' instruction. I've never performed a formal rite, much less a sacrifice.

A show, and little more. I'll send you the words, and so long as you put enough spark into the right actions, they'll love you for it.

"You have performed a ceremony before?" Jakkan asks.

"No. I left my village before Ignos gave me the chance."

Jakkan actually looks pleased at this. "The first time you hold the knife is a moment you will remember forever. You become one with the teachings. You will feel the power of Ignos as you give the greatest honor to your sacrifice. Though I must warn you: do not let the blade fall from your hands, no matter how heavy it feels. Strike with strength and make a clean cut. Ignos will be watching."

A pair of other priests enter the temple, and I stand still as they apply dyes to my face. To my shoulders and the rest of my body. Coloring me like the blue and purple cliffs. Making me the very image of dawn.

By the time they finish, Ignos is high and already a crowd gathers outside. Their murmurs and cries of deals offered and taken buzz in through the front of the Vaos. I'm not sure what to do next, so I wait for Jakkan, who, eyes closed, appears to be muttering prayers to himself.

When his lips fall still, he nods for a second, then asks me; "You are ready?"

There is only one answer to that question. "I am."

The high priest leads me from the temple, out onto the landing where the crowd, so many thousands, begins to cheer. Jakkan holds his arms high and wide, as if embracing the chants. I follow his lead, holding my arms out and soaking in the stares. The strange looks.

The mild hush that comes over the hustle and bustle as the people notice their high priest stands with another.

A woman shares his place. One, by look, not of their city or their people.

"Yes," Jakkan announces. "You have noticed that I do not take this stage alone. Beside me is a priestess. A voice of Ignos. She comes from far away, and Ignos has seen fit to pass his wisdom through her to us. Today, she will lead the sacrifice in his honor. Today we welcome this new priestess into our city. We welcome her wisdom, as it comes from Ignos himself."

The crowd stays silent for a moment. Evaluating Jakkan's words. Seeing through them, looking for the joke. Looking for a reason to disbelieve.

Now is the first chance. Tell them who you are. Strike the spark that will become the fire of their belief.

"My name is Kaishi, and I bring the heart of the jungle to this holy city. The gods have bade me bring their message to you. Ignos moves my lips and it is his words that pass from me to you. They are the words of our hope and salvation. They are the words that will bring Damantum to a new and brighter age."

Still the crowd looks wary, muttering to themselves. Until Jakkan, taking my hand in his and holding it high announces, "We honor Ignos, together."

That, at last, breaks the hold on the crowd. They cheer. Loud enough to rock the temple's foundations, or so it seems. My nerves go numb, my legs grow tight. My heart beats so fast I'm afraid it's going to burst. This, this is what my father must have felt every ceremony. This is what he had been talking about when he referred to the pulse of Ignos. His energy flowing through Father. Now, it flows through me.

Jakkan wastes no time and leads me up the steps to the very top of the Vaos. There are the twin altars, gleaming and wet from a washing earlier that morning. A pair of guards, wearing bear skins and holding their spears in one hand, stand ready. Another priest, with robes not quite as fancy as theirs, holds, on red cloth, a black-glass blade. Half as long as my arm, the mottled and jagged knife is like a shadow. Heavy, sharp. It will cut through bone as easy as through melon.

A different roar comes from below. The sacrifice has appeared, with an escort. Malo leads five guards, him wearing his lion skin. They lead their prisoner up the steps, and by the time he reaches the first landing, I recognize who it is. One of the Solare tribesmen, one of my own people that had been captured from the battle on the way here.

You can mourn him later. Do not let his sacrifice be a waste.

Now, at the foot of the Vaos, appears the boy. A man and woman, who must be his parents, form his escort. The trio marches up the steps, trailing the bowed head of the Solare prisoner. I watch, because what else can I do?

When Malo reaches me, he steps to my side and leans in close, "This is your ceremony, Kaishi. Take the honor Ignos has given you, and show it to them. We all believe. We all believe in you."

The two bear guards take the prisoner from his escort and press his back to the altar so that his head hangs off the edge. The son and his parents halt at the first landing. Beneath the part in the middle where the door to the inner chambers opens. I'm not sure why, until I notice a groove running down the center of the steps.

A funnel for the blood that leads directly to the lip of the doorway.

The blood from the prisoner will run down the stair, over the edge of the door, and onto the son. A blessing.

Do it. Claim what's rightfully ours, Kaishi.

Then Ignos speaks to me; a ritual prayer before the cutting. At first my words come quietly, but then my voice finds its stride as I recite the rite. Ignos feeds me lines, and I let them tumble from my lips. I call for honor, for blessing, for enlightenment. The greatness of the city and its people and the Emperor. At the end of it, I take the knife offered by the priest and hold it high so that Ignos catches its black-glass blade.

Then I look at the altar, at the man pressed against it. Malo, now, keeps a hand at the top of the prisoner's chest. The sacrifice's heart clear and ready. Someone has dabbed a line of red paint on the precise spot. The prisoner does not struggle. He knows, as do I and everyone else in that courtyard and on that temple, that in a moment the prisoner will come face-to-face with his god. Dying by sacrifice buys him honor, buys him a chance at a better life beyond this one.

The blade itself is heavy in my right hand. When I start to move my left hand over, so I can grip the knife with both, I see Jakkan shake his head. A priest or priestess cannot use two hands. Only one, and only precise cuts.

I place the blade against the prisoner's skin. My mouth says the words without my mind following. A last pledge to Ignos. A final call for his blessing.

I begin.

It's not the heat, or the pain that halts Sax, but rather when his foreclaws stop responding. When his legs go numb. Sax manages to look up and sees the other three Slivers have swung around. They're zeroing in on him, and the Flaum take advantage.

Their Sevora-taken minds orient the miners at Sax. Claws press in the triggers.

In their triumph, the Sevora forget to count. They don't look into the dark beyond the gateway. They don't see what's rushing towards them, mouths open and teeth glittering.

Bas gets there first. Sax sees her simply burst through a Flaum, her left and right sets of claws grabbing two more and bashing them together in front of her. The piercing fire in Sax's nerves begins to ebb, and he notices Lan, holding a pair of Flaum miners, taking easy shots at the Slivers, who have sacrificed their own dexterity to hover over Sax.

Gar, meanwhile, telegraphs his actions by way of scattered limbs and screeches. The Oratus prefers using his mouth to his tail, and any Flaum that can't run finds itself food. It's over in seconds, though Sax takes his time hauling up to his feet. His muscles spasm, and it's difficult to walk. Still, he's alive. Went right into a fight without a mask and came out the other side.

"How did it feel?" Gar asks, his face coated with evidence of terrible deeds.

"Dangerous," Sax says.

He could say more. He could talk about the thrill of knowing he was one well-placed shot away from oblivion. He could mention the blossom of fear—something he hasn't felt in a long time—when the Slivers shot him down, but the center of an enemy's ship is no place to share feelings. Gar sees he's not getting more and accepts it with a nod.

"Stupid, more like." Bas steps over the bodies to join them. "Next time, let the ones with masks take the lead."

"Odds would put our survival substantially higher than your own," Lan provides, with bits of Sliver wing hanging from her teeth. "Yet our own odds are significantly reduced should we lose you."

"I see your points." Sax gives them that, though he has no intention of waiting in the back during the next fight. No fun in it.

Together they turn towards the gateway and what lies beyond.

Much as Sax would like to take weapons, or bites, from the fight's leftovers, there's no time. If the Sevora decide to shut the door, they'll be sealed in here. So they lope to the other side.

The center ring of the seed ship is tall and thinner than the sections. A long wrap-around metal floor hugs the outside wall, providing a platform, one that is empty, much to Sax's disappointment. What's more interesting, though, is the gap between the platform and the ship's core.

It's open. A chasm that, when the four of them move forward to look, appears to vent directly into open space. The reason isn't hard to deduce: hanging above, suspended from a series of what seem to be large pipes, are ships. Small ovals, only a few times Sax's own height. They're hanging in rows of three, like teeth, with their points aiming straight down through the opening.

It's a seed ship, and they've found the seeds.

The hot soup sluices down my throat, thick and orange from the sweet potato. Across from me, Jakkan tilts his own bowl to his lips. Malo watches, sitting next to me. No bowl of his own. When I look at Malo's empty hands, Jakkan says, "This soup is for the priests. He will have his own soon enough."

"Don't worry, Kaishi." Malo throws me a smile. "It is my honor to watch over you."

It hasn't been long between the cutting of the knife and the pouring of the soup. Without looking at the sacrifice, I had spoken a final prayer and the crowd had dispersed. Returned to the ways of the day. Jakkan had then led me back into the temple, while the guards removed the body. At the base of the Vaos, the parents and their friends had celebrated the boy's ascension.

"You did well," Jakkan says, wiping away a stray trail of soup from his chin. "Your words were strong. Your grasp of the fundamentals appropriate. The flourish with the knife, they appreciated that. I do not think we should waste anymore time."

"Waste time?"

"Word came this morning," Malo says. "I've already spoken with Jakkan. It seems the Lunare are moving. Towards your jungle, and eventually us. Only they are doing something different this time; rather than killing the tribes they come across, the Lunare are pressing them into service, convincing them that the Lunare have the divine right to rule our world."

"How can they say that?" I ask.

"It doesn't matter. What it means is that we no longer have time for the voice of Ignos to perfect her training." Jakkan's sighing as he says this. "It means I don't have time to find out whether you are really telling the truth. You must prove yourself in front of the Emperor, and then in front of all our people."

"Prove what? That Ignos speaks to me? That he will tell us how to stop the Lunare?"

"We are creatures of Ignos. I said as much last night, and you saw as much today. Yet these Lunare wield magic that we have not seen. Strange devices. How do they have such things while we do not, if we are the chosen people? Our populace, even the Emperor, has begun to wonder if the Lunare are divine. If they are, in fact, what *you* claim to be."

"Jakkan knows Ignos' blessing. He can speak of his wishes. But words are as water against the hard stone of sight. See a man attacked by Viera's weapon, and your faith in Ignos' protection will be shaken," Malo says. "For those outside these city walls, especially, our hold grows tenuous."

They want you to be their tool. Take advantage of it, and when the time comes, we'll twist things around so that we're the masters.

"You want me to convince them." I follow Ignos' logic. "You want me to speak to your people and tell them what? That the Lunare are not who they say they are?"

"Declare them abominations. Affronts to Ignos. Or they will be the end of us," Jakkan says. "Do not think we are playing games here, Kaishi. Do not think that I am doing this because I want to. You must convince the Emperor, convince the people that the Lunare are nothing more than miserable things to be swept away."

"How will my words prove more effective than yours?"

"Ask," Jakkan replies. "Ask Ignos for help. Ask for his aid. If you are lying, then he will not help you and your persuasion will fail. If you are successful, however, and Ignos' gifts convince the tribes to follow the Emperor, to rise up against the enemy, then you will have saved both our people and your own."

The bracelet feels cool and heavy on my wrist. Ignos has suggested miracles lay within it. Treasures that could bring salvation to the Charre. Maybe, to my people too.

"I'll do it." There's a refreshing finality as I say this, as I choose a path to walk. "Take me to him, and I'll do everything I can to convince the Emperor. If he'll even listen to a woman like me."

"He won't listen to you, but he will listen to Ignos." Jakkan finishes his soup and sets it aside. "Now. We will take you."

I drain my bowl as Jakkan and Malo stand up. Follow them outside the Vaos, down those golden steps still wet with the remnants of the sacrifice. Walk with them to the busy streets with their hard-packed dirt, under shining afternoon light.

We head towards the Emperor's palace. I can see it, north of the Vaos and at the end of the main road. While the temple is at the center of the city, the Emperor's seat borders a lake on the north end, both a position of honor and subservience to Damantum's god.

Malo takes up a position on my left while Jakkan moves to my right. The crowds make way for us. A lion warrior, high priest and, I hear the whispers, one whom Ignos himself speaks through. Nobody troubles us. Nobody keeps their eyes on me for more than seconds. If this is celebrity, I don't mind. It feels good to be desired. To be followed.

Father had always claimed such attention required respect, that one had to earn their presence in front of the crowd.

With the sacrifice, you did so.

I keep my head high, back straight, eyes forward. Ignos' approval warms my mind.

You're becoming what you need to be. We're seeing the Emperor, and soon you'll be by his side. Eventually, you will take his place.

Take his place? Even though I, being a Solare, don't quite hold the Emperor in the same reverence as the Charre, there are stations in life. The Emperor, according to Jakkan, is chosen by divine marking, by Ignos himself. Wouldn't taking, even desiring, the Emperor's place be a direct insult to the god?

Even gods make mistakes, Kaishi. Sometimes we have to correct them.

"You must never call the Emperor by his name," Jakkan says as we walk. "You must never touch him. Not unless he commands you do so. I would advise against looking in his eyes. Or even disagreeing with him, at least directly. Rather, frame your words with respect. Understand that he is chosen not only by Ignos, but also by Damantum's people. He carries that weight in all that he does."

"Yet do not be afraid," Malo counters. "The Emperor is reasonable. He will listen to what Ignos' voice has to say."

"Malo." I suddenly want to talk of something else, keep my mind off the fact that, very soon, I would be in a room with the holiest person in the entire Charre empire. "Last night, I went to the Pits. Viera was there."

"I'm not surprised. I sold her off as soon as I left you. She's a fighter. I'm sure she did well."

"We escaped."

At Malo's look, I tell the story, and Jakkan interrupts every so often to illustrate why I had gone to the Pits in the first place. When I get to Viera's disappearance, Malo frowns.

"I take your expression to mean you don't know where she is?" I ask.

"A woman of her look will not go unnoticed in the city for long," Malo answers. "Especially one with those wounds. Wherever she is hiding, she will need food and water eventually. Then we will give Viera her reward." Malo's hand drifts to kukri hanging from his waist.

The clearing where the Emperor's palace sits is larger than the whole of my village. The palace itself could have contained our Tier inside of it. Sheer sides bleeding into a domed roof painted over with vibrant reds and yellows—core colors for Ignos. Charre prayers are carved into the walls, and many people passing by press their hands against them, muttering the same words to themselves.

A central arch leads into the palace, and two warriors, sporting lion skins like Malo's, stand guard with spears in front. The arch itself is unvarnished, beige stone without designs.

"To remind you, and all of us, of our own humility as we pass through." Jakkan answers my question. "Before we go before the Emperor, we must place ourselves beneath him, beneath Ignos."

"Incredible, isn't it?" Malo sounds swept away. "If Ignos does not love us, he would not permit this to exist."

At the entrance to the arch, after a brief inspection from the guards in which they make sure neither Jakkan nor I carry weapons, Malo puts a hand on my shoulder.

"I cannot follow you any longer. I'm not permitted inside."

"I'm going in alone?"

"Jakkan will be there."

"He's not a friend," I reply. "You are."

"Then know I will be with you in spirit." Malo laughs. "Besides, you are the messenger of Ignos, are you not? He speaks through you. With that, you are never truly alone."

How can they destroy all of the seeds? Sax is stuck on this for a minute until Bas, going past him down the metal platform, slaps her tail against the floor.

"They're not the objective," Bas says when Sax and the other two look at her. "We take the ship, they'll burn with it."

She's right, as usual, but Sax plays with his idea anyway. Bash the ships against each other and they might fall off those hooks. The gravity here is low enough that jumping up to them wouldn't be a challenge. Then they could run along the lines, torching one after the next.

It would be so much fun.

But Bas is right, so Sax follows her around the ring, looking for some path into the seed ship's core. The four of them break into a run when nothing quickly appears, because every second they spend here gives the Sevora time to regroup. Gives Avan time to figure out the mask.

They see three other gateways as they go around, all of them red-lit and locked. No paths to the central core, though. Seeds go the whole way around, minus some scattered gaps. It's hard to tell how many this one's launched, but Sax knows they'll have to hunt each of them down.

Every Sevora seed launches with a Cache, and every Cache has the specific steps to follow to bring the next wave of Sevora to power. Partly how they took over so much of the galaxy so fast—one seed ship seven cycles ago scattered Sevora around, and over time the planets they found became infested. Launched their own seed ships before anyone knew what was going on.

Now the Oratus and the rest of the free galaxy are so close. Take care of this ship, track its launches, and the Sevora would be done.

A galactic stain wiped clean.

"So what's the plan?" Lan asks when they find themselves back at their first gate.

It's easy to tell this one is where they came in, despite all four gateways being identical; the fight left plenty of splatter, and nobody has tried to clean it up.

"We have to get to the core," Sax says, though he knows this is obvious. "They must have ways of getting air and supplies to it, even if there's not a larger pathway."

"If you expect me to squeeze into one of those tubes . . ." Gar starts.

"We'll never fit," Bas says. "How about a different way? Punch in?"

"We don't have cutters with energy left," Lan reminds her, but Bas points up, towards the seeds.

"Use those," Bas says. "Take one, turn it and punch through the hull."

Sax likes the idea, but he doesn't know how to fly a seed, if they're even meant to be flown. Current thinking has the Sevora identifying possible planets and shooting the seeds out straight to their targets on autopilot.

Sax has seen cracked seeds before, and knows that there's enough nutrients packed in there that, when frozen by the sheer cold of space, a Sevora could travel as long as it needed to.

The seeds, though, aren't the only ships on this giant craft. They didn't land in the docking bay, but crashed through the lab section. Which means the Sevora must have ships elsewhere—shuttles to move their forces around, fighters to defend the seed ship. Any of those might work, any of those could crash a hole in the core.

It's a desperate move, for desperate times.

The headdress, ranging from teal to deep blue like the shallows leading out to the ocean, catches my eyes first when I enter the chamber. It sits on a cloth held by a servant; A thin man wearing only a simple cotton cape whose eyes track the floor as if it holds secrets.

Several others stand along with the man towards the back of the chamber, each one holding another treasure. Whereas the Vaos faces east and west, the palace angles north and south, so that light appears to climb in from the sides. This gives the Emperor, standing in the middle of the room, a haloed look. As though the glimmer comes from him.

Jakkan goes to the Emperor, shares a word too quiet for me to catch. The Charre's most holy person seems, to me, to be nothing more than normal. Unadorned, except for a beautiful feathered cape laced with gold, the Emperor looks no taller than my own father. His arms are thin, his face round. I see wrinkles clouding his cheeks, and his tight eyes glare at me, perhaps feeling my judgment.

"So this is the one I am supposed to respect," the Emperor announces. "The one who says she can hear from Ignos himself. Who will tell me I am wrong to think of these Lunare as gods in their own right."

Before I can reply, the Emperor strides away from Jakkan, right up to me, and his hand darts out quick and catches my chin. With one eye narrowing, the Emperor sweeps his gaze over my face, his lips twisting into a sneer, "Jakkan, I believe you've brought me the wrong one. This girl is nothing more than a scared little Solare. Out of her depth. Send her back."

Stay firm. Courage, Kaishi.

"I'm not scared," I say to the Emperor's face, and I ignore Jakkan's sudden lurch. If the high priest wants to protect me, he's too late. "I'm not out of my depth, your holiness, but exactly where I am supposed to be."

"And where is that?" the Emperor says.

"Wherever you are. So that I can relay Ignos' words directly to your ears."

"I am the holy Emperor. You presume that you need to relay Ignos' will to me?"

Brief smiles cross the lips of the servants. I notice and doubt plays its part, twinging my nerves. I'm young. Not even a Charre. What right do I have to be here, addressing the Emperor?

You have me, remember? Now tell that gilded fool that you will help him repel the Lunare.

"I cannot make you believe me," I speak slowly, measuring the words. "But I can give you secrets. Gifts from Ignos that will let us turn back the Lunare. That will give you the chance to bring the Charre to a new era of glory. All in your name."

The Emperor's face shifts into a calculating stare and I know I've found the man's weakness. He scratches at his chin for a moment, "Give me an example. Some proof of what you say."

I will tell you how Viera's weapon works, and you will tell him. Repeat my words.

"You have seen the weapons they carry? The ones that spit fire?" I ask.

I remember too—the metal and wood magic, the cracking in the valley and the Solare dropping down, dead, into the dirt.

"I have held it," the Emperor replies. "My best engineers are working even now to unveil its secrets. Though I hear the Lunare have many more, and stronger, marvels for us."

"They have the same principle. A powder that, when lit, produces an explosion that propels a rock towards its target." I'm repeating Ignos' words as they come into my head, and yet, as I say them, I understand their meaning. How Viera's weapon works unfolds itself in my mind as I narrate its function. "Your alchemists could make this powder themselves, if they so wished, and many more things besides. While outfitting an army to equal the Lunare will take time, Ignos can give you enough to scare them. To break their claim of godhood."

"Did you hear her, Jakkan?" the Emperor asks the high priest.

"I heard her well, my Emperor. I think her council wise."

"Do you? I found it strange and desperate. A girl making things up to keep herself from the altar." The Emperor raises his hand, and, as one, the servants snap to attention. "I have not grown this empire by listening to the fanciful words of jungle dwellers. Of lesser tribes. You talk of miracles, but an Emperor must deal in realities. I—"

"Please, holiness," Jakkan says to the Emperor's back. "What cause have we to ignore Kaishi's advice? The people have heard her message and approve of it. If she is correct, and Ignos really can help us through her, then what have we to lose?"

The Emperor considers me, and I can see a twisting anger there, mingling with the slightest hint of fear. The Emperor, holiest of holies, believes me a threat. The realization travels up and down my soul like lightning. If the Emperor finds me dangerous, then my only future is under the knife.

He will change his mind. Everyone in this room heard your words. Everyone in this room heard the high priest support you. Not even the Emperor can kill one so obviously favored by Ignos without repercussions.

Speak what I say again, and we may yet get out of this alive.

I sink to my knees, press my forehead to the cool stones in front of the Emperor in his feathered, gold cape. "I swear to you, Emperor, that we will have the tools you need by the time the Lunare near. They will be awed by your brilliance, by the power of your people, and you will chase their armies to the ends of the world."

I don't look up until I feel the Emperor's touch on my shoulder. The servants and the guards relax. Looking down at me, the Emperor speaks, "You promise much, Solare, but Jakkan vouches for you. So I shall give you your workers. You shall have until the Lunare pass Tutio. If you fail, then your life will be given to Ignos, and Jakkan will lie beside you, his heart carved first."

Sax relays the crash-into-the-core idea to the set, and there's cautious agreement. Theoretically, Sax's plan holds up, though there's a lot of ifs. Still, nobody has a better idea, so Sax gets the vote to go.

"I don't know which gateway leads to the docking bay," Sax says after, and even Bas shakes her head.

"Why suggest it then?" Bas replies. "We don't have time to explore every section on this ship."

"Then we start with the closest one." Another bit of Vincere code: When in doubt about what to do, complete the simplest action first. Since nobody knows which way is right, they ought to go the first way they can.

Of course, the next gateway is locked. Sax glares at the black nub as it scans for Sevora and finds none. It's not intimidated. How to break through a door when they have no weapons? Above them, a rushing noise echoes from the pipes. All four Oratus scatter, on instinct, to minimize the impact of an attack.

Lan points her miner up, but doesn't fire because there isn't any target. Sax traces the noise along the pipes to the nearest rank of seed ships, which start to shake.

They're being filled.

The seeds settle, and a steady, growing thrum replaces the rushing noise. Sax watches the seeds vibrate, and suddenly the row of three near them begins to steam. Loud whines echo through the ring as engines spin up, and the noise answers the question of why nobody's in here. If this happens regularly, Sax would lose his hearing, and shortly thereafter, his mind.

Then a seed drops. It's a slow thing due to the gravity, but the hook, with the piping running through the barb to the back of the seed, retracts. After a couple moment's fall to clear the hook, the seed's engine pulses into full ignition. Fire pushes back up towards the pipes, white-hot, and then the seed is down and gone, through whatever shield the Sevora put between vacuum and the ship's air, and out to space.

The second and third seed follow seconds later, and Sax is left with a ringing head and a dangerous idea. "We use the seeds," Sax says to the set, and they hiss in laughter.

"I want to see you fly one," Bas says, knowing full well Sax hasn't flown a ship in his life.

But Sax is ready. For once, he has a comeback to Bas and her knowing sarcasm. Rather than trust his words, though, Sax turns around and leaps. He goes high, up to the nearest seed, and hits it.

Sticks his claws into its shell. It's not cloth, but few things can handle an Oratus digging in, and he finds purchase.

"What are you doing?" Gar shouts from below.

"Aiming!" Sax edges his way around the seed, setting each claw in before he moves the next, until he's gone halfway around.

The other two seeds in the row are behind him now, and in front, below, is the gateway. Now that he's listening for it, Sax hears the rushing noise, only this time feeding into a different part of the ring. The seed ship is launching again. Maybe in desperation, maybe because it can. Either way, Sax bets that these seeds will fire soon.

So he presses in with his claws and leaps, turning in the air, to the next seed. Catches himself. Now he has leverage. Sax, with his left claws biting deep into the second seed, leans out and looks at the three Oratus.

"Two more!" Sax shouts, a raspy, ear-splitting hiss. "Together, we can push it."

This hits the others like inspiration. Bas and Gar win a battle of glances and copy Sax's flight. They scramble around the first seed, and, with Sax descending to the pointed front of the second seed, get themselves in position.

"When it starts to fall," Sax says. "You'll jump. Gar, you go first. Then Bas. I'll go last."

The three of them are on the seed when the fluid starts rushing again. As Sax hopes, it's coming right above them this time. Burbling, roaring and flushing down into the seed. Sevora likely pouring in with it. Ready to launch and infect some unlucky world.

This one, at least, won't be getting to its destination.

"Ready," Sax says. Bas and Gar hiss in agreement.

The seed starts to shake. Both the one they're on, and their target. If it goes like before, the target will fall first, and that will give the Oratus their chance.

The right hook moves. It shakes, begins to lift off of the first seed and Sax doesn't have to say anything for Gar to know his time is now.

Gar leaps, pressing off with his claws and lunging towards the first seed as it falls loose from the hook. Bas follows. They both hit the seed as it starts to fall. The force of their leap couples with the low gravity to shove the seed towards the gateway, into prime position for Sax to make his own jump. He presses his legs, digs deep and angles towards the front point, that bottom apex of the seed.

And leaps.

He leads with his shoulders, trying to push every ounce of force he has into the seed as he strikes it. A loud roar starts in the ring; the seed's engines igniting. As Sax hits, he notices Gar and Bas dropping away, beginning their slow fall to the metal floor. Sax himself feels the seed rotate, their combined impact is enough to orient the craft.

Sax holds the nose as it swings up, and then he feels himself accelerate. The seed is moving, its engines launching the ship right towards the gateway.

Sax can't hang on. His momentum will send him right into the same spot as the seed. So he pushes off, down towards the floor, and away from the gateway.

Only it's too far. His momentum too much. He's overshooting; falling into the chasm that leads to outer space. Sax twists in the air, staring down at the black emptiness beneath him. Nothing out there but cold death.

The noises of the second and third seeds beginning their own release rumble up, and then a shattering bang, a crashing crumble of metal and dust and sparks as the seed they pushed hits . . . something.

Sax can't tell, as he's drifted below the floor and all he can see are the launching seeds starting their path towards him.

"Flip your tail up!" Bas's voice, and Sax follows her instructions without thinking. That's the point of a pair: you do what they ask without doubt because it will save your life.

He feels claws bite into his tail and it hurts, but Sax stops falling. There's a lurch and someone's pulling him back. He feels the heat as the next seed closes on him. Even if the seed doesn't hit him directly, its rockets will burn Sax to ash.

"Hurry!" Sax hisses.

There are honorable ways to die. There are deaths full of pride, like sacrificing yourself to harm the enemy. Giving your last breath to one more swipe of the claws. This would not be one of those. This would be sad. Pathetic.

The pull increases, and Sax bumps against the side of the chasm and then back over the metal floor as the seed brushes past behind him. The skin of his head puckers at the heat, his scales blister, but Sax lives.

It's Lan holding Gar, holding Bas, who pulls Sax back up. He lives because they work together as a set. He lives because the Oratus do not abandon each other. But none of them mention it. They don't have to. They all know their job and they do it.

Now they're looking at the wrecked hole where the gateway used to be. The seed ship isn't even there. It punched right through. Hard rock meant to last for cycles in space, propelled by rocket engines, is more than enough for an interior gateway.

On the other side, they see something Sax never expects. Something he didn't think the Sevora capable of.

Malo leads us back towards the Vaos as Ignos dips towards the horizon, but we've barely left the Emperor's presence before the high priest whispers in my ear, "Tell me of these miracles you wish to produce, and I will see the proper people informed."

Kaishi, the real power is yours now. Don't give it up.

"No, Jakkan." I stop in the middle of the street, forcing the high priest to do the same. Ignos is right. The Emperor put my life against the success of these miracles, and I will not leave their success up to Jakkan. "You will bring the people I ask to me, and I will inform them of the tasks myself. This is my duty to the Emperor, and Ignos works through me."

"Kaishi," Jakkan slides a smile onto his face. A warm one, understanding. "You must realize that you are an outsider. The artisans you need will not work with a Solare, no matter how much she says her words are those of Ignos himself."

"Then you," and I look at Malo, sharing him in my words. "And Malo will make them. Or I will tell the Emperor his miracles have been lost because his own people will not follow his orders."

Jakkan's warm smile vanishes, replaced by a tight line. Malo, meanwhile, appears uncertain, looking at Jakkan and I. Even people passing around us glimpse the tension and give a wide berth.

"Your tone has changed, Kaishi," Jakkan says. "Have I not said that we must be allies here to save our civilization? That we must work together?"

There had been a time when a promise of friendship would have swayed my heart. My mind, even. Now, in the cold crush of Damantum's people, surrounded by buildings instead of trees, with the burning smell of forges instead of soft flowers, my soul keeps its clarity. I observe Jakkan's words like I would a strange insect, searching for their true intent.

I find nothing kind in them.

"Together," I reply, memories of the Pits and Jakkan's first, lethal task driving heat into my words. "Yes. Only as partners now, not with my body under your foot."

"He is the high priest, Kaishi," Malo pleads. "Second only to the Emperor himself. Please."

Jakkan nods at the warrior, his eyes still on mine. Waiting for me to break and submit.

You were beneath them, now you are equal. Soon you will be greater. We're nearly there, Kaishi.

"Partners." I don't smile. "Call me whatever you wish, but either we are equals, or this city can burn."

Jakkan sinks into a look I've seen before on Father's face; one of calculation. Schemes brew behind Jakkan's wrinkled, leathery skin. I see scenarios play out, each one twisting in the high priest's mind until he comes out ahead.

"As partners." Jakkan nods at last. "For the city, and our people, I will set aside my pride. As you have failed to do."

I ignore the bait. I have the status I want, now I need the loyalty. "Do you still believe in me, Malo?"

"If I did not, then I would not be here, priestess," Malo replies, though the words come less ready than before. A sign, perhaps, that the warrior is less than happy with my grasp of power.

A true leader cannot be overly concerned with the feelings of her subjects. They will follow you, and that is enough.

"Then here are the people I would see." I pull the list from Ignos, and I feel the Cache burn on my wrist as he calls to it. Images and formulas full of symbols I don't recognize pour through my mind and it's all I can do to keep from screaming right there. I think, without the sacrifice and its pressure to train me, I would have. "The city's best workers of metal and wood. Damantum's greatest jewelers and alchemists. Bring them all to me, and we'll begin the work needed to fight off the Lunare."

"I can see to that," Jakkan starts, but I cut him off.

"No, Jakkan. While Malo gathers the people, you and I have to do something more important," I look down at myself, and then point at Jakkan's own robe and headdress. "I need clothes, jewels like your own. I must be more than a priestess. I must be what Ignos would desire of his messenger. Make me look the part."

The high priest does not dispute the argument. Instead, as Malo departs to arrange discussions with the city's premier artisans, Jakkan takes me on a tour of Damantum's markets. With the high priest at my side, the shopkeepers don't look away as they did before. Zolin, tending to his plants, notices with a start that I'm still alive. I give him a smile and he shakes his head.

First, I have to choose a color. As the Emperor embodies the blues of seas and shallows, and Jakkan uses the reds of blood and soil, so I need to choose shades that will set my soul into my clothes, hair, and skin.

It's not a hard decision.

"The luminous greens of the jungle," I announce to the dyers, whose stands are cluttered with pots containing all manner of colored inks. "I want to shimmer like an emerald, but with the mystery of a forest valley."

Second, a headdress. My crown. A band with feathers or stalks;

straight threads of colors. Again, I'm drawn to my roots. The shades of the birds around my village: black and white and yellow. A burst of orange and red for fruits and flowers. The craftsmen begin sticking feathers, dyed and not, into a band. The resulting arrangement, while holding the appropriate hues, appears jangled.

"That will not match your green cape," Jakkan whispers as we look at the initial attempt.

"Why should I care?" I reply. "I'm supposed to represent all people, Charre and Solare. Different colors seem the easiest way to do that."

"A fair argument," Jakkan says. "Yet, as one knowledgeable about such things, remember that the people see you as you are, not as you wish to be. They will wonder why you choose such a strange arrangement, they will ask why a messenger of Ignos seems so ugly, why her headdress stands so apart from the others Ignos favors."

Jakkan may have a point, Kaishi. This thing you have created is, shall I say, quite unappealing to the eyes.

I want to push back. Want to be stubborn, but Ignos' voice meshes with Jakkan's appeals—which, this time, hold no trace of another agenda—and I back down, "You might be right. Let's try a bright green in the center declining towards black at the edges."

Even the craftsman is more excited about this than my first attempt, and the end product shows it. When I place the crown on my head and stare at myself in the still basin of water kept at the stand for that purpose, the headdress is a vibrant, verdant green. As if life itself has come from above and traced its way down to me.

"Beautiful," Jakkan says, and I think he means it. "Now, there is one place left for you to visit."

Similar to the dyers, the tattoo artists have bowls of various inks around their stands. Stones serve as chairs, with warriors and others sitting on them while the artists perform their work, creating intricate inkings of Ignos, lions, bears, and the Vaos.

Jakkan, shifting his cape so that I can see the elaborate design dominated by Ignos on his back, says, "Here you must pick your new body. Your old one will be given to Ignos. Open yourself to his wisdom, and let his words guide your tongue in the telling, and their hands in the painting."

I wait for Ignos to tell me what I should do. How I can transform my own body into a powerful message, but Ignos is silent. I sit on the stone, feel the cool, rough rock against my thighs, and think. Jakkan and the artist, an old, weathered man, stare at me.

If I have to choose for myself, then, there is one design fit for my body. One depicting the god that has brought me this far. That has done so much to change my life. I describe the details: The light green shades. A circular design with a wide set of eyes in the middle; an everlasting search for knowledge. Four arrows reaching out from the center, to look in all directions. At the angles, carved blocks to serve as the foundations that same knowledge created. At the end, a series of circles filling in the gaps: the travel of ideas from discovery to practice.

Ignos, a part of my mind, will now be part of my body as well. While I speak, the artist dips and pierces. Pokes and paints my skin. There is pain, yes, but I bear it, because there is no other option.

One step closer, Kaishi. One step closer to the salvation of your people.

It's dark, but not total, and not sinister.

Rather, what Sax sees now is a luminous show that uses the shadows to focus the eyes on what they're meant to see. Which, in this case, are glorious fountains: arches of water spritzing back and forth over vast areas covered in what Sax can only describe as entertainment.

Tables, mobbed by Flaum, Teven, Whelks and other species Sax is not able to recognize from afar, blink and flash through various games. Pulsating beats clash and echo across the metal flooring, and every thud carries with it a multitude of cries and calls. Floating banners move back and forth through the space, illuminating with advertisements and movies.

"We found their fun," Lan says, and she's right.

Seed ships hold many thousands, and it now seems obvious to Sax that to keep even Sevora in a civil state, there has to be a way for them to enjoy themselves. A place to go when not on shift, a place to have fun. To cavort, to play games and remind themselves that all is not one battle after the next.

The Sevora need this because they are weak. Because they cannot handle the cruel reality of life.

Sax also sees the seed, or what remains of it. It's punched through the gateway and lies on the ground in front of them. At the bottom of the steps and further beyond, having, it looks like, bounced its way to its final resting place: burrowed into the side of what had once been some sort of lit statue, which is now sparking.

Sevora species gather around it, pointing and chattering. All of which means nobody is noticing the gateway or the four Oratus standing there, haloed by the bluish light of the center ring behind them.

"Let's use it," Sax says. "Keep moving. Remember mauling these Sevora isn't the objective. We need to get back to the outer ring, to the docking bay."

"If it's even in this section," Gar says.

"If it's not, then we'll try another," Bas replies.

"If it takes that long, I may have to eat some Flaum," Gar mutters as they start their walk.

Every foot fall onto the hard floor brings new assaults to Sax's senses. He sees Flaum in various states of intoxication. Falling over each other, or simply standing with glassed eyes and slack expressions on their faces. A reckless sloth that would never be permitted on a Vincere ship. Slivers alight on posts covered with purchase for their talons. They too seem exhausted. Uncaring of the four Oratus wandering in their midst.

Sax thinks he knows why.

They're so deep in the seed ship now. So far beyond the outside, that what are the odds of an enemy force making it here? It's far more likely that these four Oratus are taken, Sevora slaves like the rest of them. Though even if they weren't, Sax is fairly sure these creatures wouldn't mind. They are so far removed from real consciousness that Sax thinks they wouldn't react if he begins carving them up right here in the open.

So they keep going. Into and through the center of the section, which is a large square with a bursting sapphire fountain in the middle, one that seems to spray up different colored water. Around it, spread at intervals, are vast arrays of tables and chairs and nutrient dispensing machines. Most of the spots are taken with Sevora-hosted species happily munching away on whatever they can get.

"Fascinating, isn't it?" Sax knows the voice. Turns and sees Avan, no longer wearing any of his armor, watching them. The captive Oratus has apparently made his way out of the dark crowd. Avan spreads his claws wide, as if to show he means no harm. "Please, let me speak."

Sax sees, or rather feels, Gar twitch, crouch down into an attacking stance. They can't afford a battle here, so Sax whacks Gar with his tail.

"We're in enemy territory," Sax hisses as Gar snarls back at him. "You start a fight here, we'll never survive."

Gar keeps his glare hot, but lowers his claws.

Avan clasps his own in front of him. "You're right of course. With one yell, I could have a horde descend upon you. You would doubtless slay many, but you would be torn apart." He pauses, his vents taking in a long breath. "You and I both know the small fleet you have at this end of the galaxy won't destroy this seed ship for a very long time. How many more worlds will the Sevora infect before you bring it down?"

"Wherever you go, we will find you and we will end you," Sax replies. He desperately wants to do as Gar nearly did: tear Avan's grin off of his face.

"I'm sure," Avan replies. "But what if I told you it won't matter? What if I told you that there are things you don't know. Things that would make your every action meaningless, if you knew them?"

"Why haven't you killed us yet?" Sax hisses the only question that matters—if Avan's tracked them here, then he could have shot them, stunned them or burned them.

He's done none of those things.

"Because I want to leave," Avan says. "I need a way off of the seed ship, and I need a way to survive. You are that way. An offer: I will guide you to a ship, to your chance at the glory you so desperately seek, if you will guarantee me safe passage back to your own vessel."

"How do you know we're looking for the docking bay?" Bas asks.

"Because you are on a seed ship. They hear everything. I hear everything."

Sax flexes his claws. "Then why are you talking to us now? Revealing your plan?"

Avan looks around at the loud, thumping surroundings. "They can hear everything, except for this place. Except for where there's so much noise that the recorders catch only garbled nonsense. Where it's so dark and difficult to see that it's hard to know what's happening."

"But we only came here by chance," Lan argues. "You couldn't have known that—"

"By chance?" Avan interrupts. "Who do you think triggered the seed ships to launch? Who do you think waited until you derived your plan and made sure the right ones fired when you were ready? Which, thank you for making it so much easier than I had expected. Crashing through the gateway with a seed ship? None of us saw that coming."

Avan has them. Sax knows this. They can either go with him, or fight him here and now. Though Sax can't tell, he assumes Avan's figured out how to put on the mask. Which means he's protected, to some degree. The four of them could likely make an end of him, but then their own deaths would come shortly thereafter.

Or they could trust the despicable creature and follow him to the docking bay. To where they wanted to go.

"I don't think we have a choice," Sax hisses. He waits for a denial, but none comes.

Though he hates the razor smile that pulls over Avan's face, Sax does nothing to erase it.

The meetings with Damantum's premier artisans and craftsmen are, according to the Emperor, to begin immediately. With my outfits determined, Jakkan leaves me back at the Vaos, which, he says, will serve as my home.

Kaishi, now's the time. The Cache. Use it.

The bracelet. Green and shimmering in the light. I run my fingers along its warm sides. It flashes, and I feel as though the light streams through my eyes and into my core.

The Cache stores our knowledge, Kaishi. Make miracles with it. Give your people what they need.

Using the Cache feels like reaching through my own memories, only the things I find are like nothing I've ever seen before. Pictures of creatures I don't recognize from any legend, places so beautiful and terrible they defy description. And things. Wonders that Ignos promises will change the course of my world. I begin to fall, diving through one after another. There is so much to see, and I want to learn it all!

Stop.

Ignos' voice pierces my frantic churning. The image in my mind shifts to something that looks like Viera's weapon.

The Cache holds too many secrets for any one person. Look for what you need, and you'll find it. Look for everything, and that is what you will lose.

From that point until, with night long descended, Malo returns with the first group of artisans, Ignos and I explore the Cache. We pick out miracles suitable for the Charre; ones that can be built in the time, and with the materials, that we have. I choose several more too, ones Ignos thinks are beyond us, but that I believe will stoke the fires of our imaginations. Belief in the new powers coming to us.

Yes. You must think of the Charre, now, as your people. That is what they will become, soon.

Are they my people? The Charre, who took me from my home? I don't think so, but then, I can't afford to treat them as enemies. To do so means death. I know that if the Charre can push back the Lunare, then perhaps I can persuade them to leave my own village alone, to protect them.

So I stand ready to begin when Malo enters the temple.

First there are the metalworkers, and with them I show schematics. How to make the magic fire that Viera had summoned so effortlessly. How to make even larger weapons, ones that could shoot hundreds or thousands of projectiles in mere moments of time.

Not all of them are possible with Damantum's workshops, and even if the Charre had the material, knowing the plans and executing them are two different things.

Still, we speak, with Malo fueling us with tea throughout the night and into the next day. The metalworkers have their own ideas, looking at what the Cache provides, and leave with the coming of dawn to produce their own versions of Ignos' miracles.

I barely have time to blink before the next group arrives.

The woodworkers. I give them designs for boats and larger ships, even planes that will fly through the air. I show things that are so far beyond their greatest imagining, seeing my own legend building in their eyes. Creating a priestess that has all the answers. That has all the guidance for what is to come. The woodworkers leave like the metalworkers, with visions dancing through their minds and inspiration pouring from their mouths.

The doctors follow a quick lunch of peppers and pork. We go over detailed maps of cells and biology, though I'm disappointed to learn the Cache holds no diagrams of our own species. Regardless, in several hours of conversation, the entire medical practice of the Charre people transforms.

Word spreads of the miraculous priestess hiding in the Vaos. Jakkan begins functioning as my own assistant. Scheduling meetings, making sure I'm adequately cared for. Ushering in and out groups of all kinds. From writers to hunters, sculptors to warriors. All of them come. All of them ask for more. I, with Ignos in my mind, am only too happy to give them everything I can.

This. This is how you find your people. This is where everything you are becomes real. Where the Charre stop looking to the Emperor, and start looking to you.

I don't dare put that thought to words.

Not even the Emperor himself is immune to the rumors. On the third day, he calls for another audience. I go, with Jakkan, back to the palace. Back to see the Emperor in all his finery. Again he stares at me and issues warning after warning, threat after threat. He expresses fear and angst over the Lunare, who are taking their time in approaching. They are gathering up smaller tribes with their own wonders. Claims are spreading that the Lunare are the true gods. That Ignos favors them.

The Emperor throws us back to the streets with demands, ones that I plan to exceed.

By the fourth and fifth days, as evidence of my miracles becomes known on the streets, as the first objects coming from my teachings find their way to the Emperor, his opinions change. On the sixth, when the Emperor calls, he does not request Jakkan. This time, Malo asks only for me.

This time, I go to the Emperor alone.

With nobody there to help me, other then the voice of Ignos in my head, I promise the Emperor that I will deliver. That my wonders will be ready. That when the two of us go out to greet the Lunare, the sheer brilliance of the many inventions of the Charre people given to them by Ignos will not only bring all of the other tribes to their knees, they will bring the Lunare themselves to heel.

The Lunare, I promise, will realize their mission is a hopeless one. They will leave in fear. The Emperor will rightfully reign over all.

Rather than issue his customary defensive threats, the Emperor reaches behind him, to a servant who holds a small box. From it he pulls out a small thing that looks like a tube with a wooden leg on the end. Like the weapon Viera had held. The Emperor points it at the far wall. Presses back on the lip of metal sticking up from the top. And then pulls another small loop of metal with his finger.

The noise inside the palace is deafening. A loud crack reverberates from the stones and pierces my ears. I'm stunned, my head rings and I do all I can to stop myself from diving onto the ground or running away. Only the Emperor, watching me to see what I do, keeps me from it.

When I manage to look, I see a chunk of the stone wall is missing; crumbled on the floor. The Emperor stares at the device.

"Your miracles are more than just words," the Emperor says. "This, this is what we need. This will make the difference. We cannot, unfortunately, make enough. We do not have the mines. The forges. Yet."

"We will, your Holiness," I say. "In time, yours will be the mightiest nation ever known to man."

"Perhaps," the Emperor replies. "But will we have that time?"

I don't know how to answer, and the Emperor, placing the weapon back in the box, doesn't seem to expect me to.

"The Lunare have many of these. Some longer, larger. I am told they have whole roving monstrosities covered in large things they call cannons that, when fired, sound as though the sky is being ripped asunder. How can your miracles compete with this?"

"They can be better. They will be better. But we need time."

"Does Ignos tell you how to find that?"

Meet them. Go out, confront the Lunare face-to-face. Scare them. Take the wonders we have, and use them to buy that time. Every day, every week you get is crucial.

"We can't let them reach the city," I say. "If they do, they can disrupt our efforts. They can distract the people that are even now working to put these devices together. You are the holiest, Emperor. With me by your side, we can change the minds of the tribes that follow the Lunare. We can tell the Lunare they are no longer welcome, and show enough to prove it."

The Emperor's hand reaches up and brushes his headdress, fingers filtering through the feathers, "Ignos has seen fit to guide you this far, and I would be foolish not to follow the wisdom he shares through you. Perhaps it is time for us to reveal ourselves. Get ready, for tomorrow, we shall make for the desert and show the Lunare they never should have left the mountains."

42 / WHO LIVES AND DIES

With Avan leading them, Sax and the others make their way out of the entertainment section. Plenty of Sevora stare at the group of five Oratus, though they turn to their drinks quick enough after a glare or a wave of a menacing claw. Like the gateway in the central ring, green lights halo the exit from this section, further out from the core.

Looking back, Sax sees the broken gateway already under repair. The crashed ship already cleared. Entertainment section or no, the Sevora could move fast when they wanted to.

"Tell me," Sax says to Avan as the latter raises his head to the next gateway's scanners. "How many Sevora are on this ship?"

"Thousands," Avan replies, not turning away from the black nub. The green lights blink and the gateway shunts open. "Enough to rotate crews around continuously. Those behind us are enjoying their time off."

"Even in the middle of a battle?"

"We have been at war constantly for cycles. If we hadn't found a way to find joy in the midst of all the fighting, we would be a sad species indeed." Avan wraps his long mouth into a smile. "Although I suppose you Oratus don't quite understand that."

"The battle is our joy," Gar says.

"Yes. Of course it is." Avan waves them through.

This section feels more like a labyrinth, with narrow corridors between tall walls that stretch from floor to ceiling. Circular windows dot those walls, and, going by the large doors appearing every so often with keypads, Sax assumes these are the homes for Sevora living on the ship. Capsules for sleeping and little more.

On the sides of the structures, spidering out over the pathways, are perches on black metal poles. Slivers land on them, wrapping their bodies around the bars for rest. Yellow lamps hang from these perches like fruit from trees, spreading soft light across the cold metal floor. Every so often they walk through small plots of plants in cutouts between buildings, a brief concession to beauty in an otherwise efficient design.

The entertainment section held swarms of Sevora shifting around. Mobs of them cackling with laughter or sharing meals. Here, though, what Sevora they see—in the usual assortment of Flaum, Teven, and Whelk hosts—travel by themselves or in pairs. Rushing, always. As if being caught outside here would result in something terrible. Avan, who doesn't say anything as they walk through the district, seems to sense Sax's impending question and looks back at him.

"This section is currently under resting orders," Avan said. "Species are only to be moving through here in emergencies, which is why you're seeing worried looks. As you might imagine, keeping our workforce healthy is of paramount importance."

He points a claw towards one of the windows up above. "From the outside, these are designed to only cast light frequencies that promote sleep. On the inside, there are screens showing images that promote relaxation. A variety of substances are also available to help Sevora find the rest they require."

"You drug your own people?" Bas says. Sax flashes to the Stim he took at the start of this mission, but keeps quiet.

Avan turns fully around as they reach a point between buildings, where a single arch plant, its many pink curling vines twisting up and over each other, provides decoration. "To think that a species as oblivious as yours is besting us in this war . . . yes. We do. Neither Flaum nor Teven are natives to space, and they, being quick to mature and easy to dominate, make up the majority of our forces. In order to ensure the hosts get the required rest in an environment not conducive to such things, we use various means."

"Not only are you taking their bodies, but you are ruining them as well?" Lan says. "And you hope the rest of the galaxy will let you live?"

The rest of them hiss agreement—Sax too. Avan must be under the influence of his own drugs to think the Oratus would agree to share the galaxy with a species like this.

"You say that as if we Sevora can control who, what we are," Avan replies, taking Lan's provocation in stride. He spreads his four arms wide, expanding the claws. "We need hosts to survive. Few Sevora ever reach full maturation and the capability to breed—to do so requires space and protection, which we haven't seen for cycles. As such, we . . . copy ourselves. Grow new Sevora in tubes and pools. Yet still, we number far less than the ubiquitous Flaum, who pollute the galaxy with their trillions."

Pollute the galaxy. An interesting phrase, if not entirely wrong. Sax has seen more than his share of Flaum on Vincere ships, and they tend to be the first to come and rebuild worlds rescued from the Sevora grip. Flaum produce litters numbering close to a dozen or more. Enough so that pairs of Flaum could repopulate cities on their own in little time. If the species possessed the intelligence or strength to make their own attempt at ruling the galaxy, the Flaum would have little trouble achieving dominance through sheer numbers alone.

"You need to find the benefits," Sax says as Avan recommences their march. "Why should we let the Sevora continue to exist? What good do you provide?"

Avan doesn't have an answer ready. No eloquent argument or sharp comeback. After walking in silence, after they leave the capsules behind and come to the next gateway, only then does Avan stop short of the scanner and glance at Sax, his eyes burning.

"Who are you to play as gods, and decide what species live or die?"

It's not long after the meeting with the Emperor when, back at the Vaos, two guards come in looking for me. They're wearing bear skins, and when Jakkan asks why they're here, they point to me. "We have information for the high priestess."

"High priestess?" Jakkan says, and while I pick up the surprise, Jakkan doesn't flinch.

"As the Emperor has decreed she is to be addressed," one guard says. I try to look at Jakkan, to say I have nothing to do with this, but the high priest doesn't look at me.

"Then address her." Jakkan turns back to a scroll he's reading.

"What is it?" I ask.

"We've captured a Lunare," the guard begins. "Hiding in the city. Apparently, she had made threats to a family, secured a room in their house. But she has since fallen ill, and now she begs for your help."

"Viera," I say, and I catch Jakkan's ears perk up at the name. "Where is she?"

"We have her chained at the foot of the temple," the warrior replies. "We are ready to prepare her for sacrifice. It does not look as though she will live much longer, so we should hurry."

"Bring her in," I order. It feels strange to do that. To command someone.

You are powerful now. It is only right that you use what you've gained. And that what you've gained will change who you are.

"In?" the guard seems confused.

"In here. In this chamber. I made a promise to the woman, and Ignos will not see it broken."

At the mention of the god, the two guards stamp their spears and vanish.

"So your friend has returned." Jakkan's voice is heavy with warnings. "I would advise you to be careful. The Lunare are not well-liked in the city, as you can well imagine. Being seen helping one will not do you any favors."

"I can only hope that the miracles Ignos has given will buy me enough respect to help Viera," I reply, then, after thinking for a moment. "My tribe did not try to fight every one that came through our territory. There is a chance that the Lunare don't have to be your enemy. They could be valuable traders. Partners even. We just have to convince our people."

"Kaishi, it is not us you have to convince," Jakkan says. "It's the Lunare and their band of marauders. If they wish to trade and return to their mountains, we would gladly barter with them. What they want, however, cannot be traded. Only taken."

Before I can reply, the guards bring in their captive. It is Viera, though far paler, sweating, and unconscious. The problem isn't hard to spot: the wounds I cauterized, those white marks scarring her chest and arms, are red and inflamed around the edges. Rashes span across the front of her body.

Infection.

There are ways to cure this. Though none that you currently possess.

I implore Ignos to tell me more. I'd made a promise to Viera. Also, given Jakkan's increasingly askance looks, and the Emperor's otherworldly standing, I have few friends in the city. If there is any way to keep Viera alive, I want to use it.

Then here's what you must gather.

Ignos rattles off a series of ingredients. Instructions for how to blend and cook them together. To make a small pile of powder, stuff that I would need to keep on making until the infection subsides. I tell Jakkan, and I can see his reluctance to help me gradually gives in to the desire to see another miracle in action.

We dispatch the guards to find herbalists and glass workers, while Jakkan and I stoke a large fire. In the hours between the guards departing and returning, I lay Viera down, and use a cool cloth to wet her forehead. To try and calm the fever raging inside her.

Viera utters words in her own language, twisting and turning on the floor. Sweat drenches her, and her pallor grows. It's obvious that she won't live long.

"A sacrifice will not break your promise," Jakkan says at one point while I'm matting the cloth on Viera's forehead. "You made that vow to a living, healthy woman. Now, she's dying. You have the opportunity to honor her. You have the chance to have her depart this earth and go to the home she so obviously wishes to return to. Give her to Ignos, Kaishi. Gain the people's everlasting love."

Jakkan speaks wisdom. Get what you can from those you can use. Don't spend your influence on a lost cause.

I can't.

There simply isn't a part of me that can accept carving into Viera's chest and pulling out her heart. Not after I'd worked so hard to keep her alive. Not after she'd helped me from the juar pit.

No.

I will save her, or she will die in the attempt.

Using the Cache, I walk the herbalists through the process. The steps to turn these ordinary ingredients into medicine that will give Viera a chance. Metal, herbal leaves, the fermented alcohol that would otherwise be used to make honeyed wine, all of these and more are boiled together until they form a strange milky substance.

Then, I spread it on the infection.

We repeat the same process for three days. Each time I whisper to Viera that she will get better. That she will soon be up and running again. It helps me believe, if nothing else.

Caring for Viera does not, of course, take all of my time. I still work with Damantum's artisans, checking and advising them on their progress. Testing what they develop. Learning from their expertise and coupling it with the secrets the Cache provides.

Until the Emperor himself appears at the Vaos.

I've been turning away his messengers every morning, declaring that I cannot leave yet. It's one thing to tell a meek servant that I'm too busy working miracles to depart the city. It's another thing to see the Emperor in full regalia stride up and into the chamber, to see Jakkan fall to his knees and bow. I copy him, if only because the Emperor's expression tells me my life depends, now, on subservience.

"I'm told the march to save my people waits on one woman," the Emperor's voice, in the close confines of these chambers, echoes off the walls. "I'm told that my priestess, the one that promised salvation for the Charre, lets the Lunare gather their strength, lets them draw closer . . ."

The Emperor strides, as he trails off, between Jakkan and I, over to where Viera lays on her mat, still unconscious, if not quite so pale as before.

"For this one. A Lunare herself—"

"A friend," I say, standing and ignoring Jakkan's muted gasp. "A friend who saved me when none of your own would. Who protected me as I now protect her."

The Emperor reaches to his waistband, pulls out a black-glass knife from a loop. His face is blank as he holds the knife out to me.

The implication is clear.

I refuse it.

The Emperor pulls the knife back slow. Gives me plenty of time to reconsider, but I stand firm. As Ignos says, I am powerful now. I have the weight of miracles on my side. And I choose to use that weight for what I believe is right.

"If you will not sacrifice this one," the Emperor says, and I'm relieved when he slips the knife back into his loop, "then we will take her with us. The Lunare are at Tutio, and we have no more time to wait."

"Take her with us?" I'm too surprised by the statement to watch my own words.

"I have had a cart prepared. It waits at the steps, along with several priests to care for her." The Emperor looks at Viera.

"Then you planned for this from the start?"

"One Lunare is not worth risking my high priestess's support," the Emperor replies, but when I start to thank him, he talks over me. "Do not make me regret this. Prepare her to move, and let us save my people."

Ships of all sizes spread out across the docking bay, visible from the gateway as Sax and the others go through behind Avan. Rather than only a magnetic shield, as with the seeds, here a large, sliding set of metal plates act as an additional layer of protection. Each plate interlocks with the ones next to it through sliding latches. Even now, Sax sees one of the plates slide back and a pair of Sevora space fighters—dart-shaped things with a single, cylindrical energy cannon on the nose—jet out into the dark.

Sax estimates another dozen or more fighters sitting behind those two, though pilots didn't seem to be lining up to fly. The seed ship is in the middle of a pitched fight, where it has been boarded by an enemy force, and it hasn't launched all of its defenses?

"Why?" Sax asks Avan. "What are all of these ships still doing here?"

Avan keeps moving, heading down onto the vast flat section. Sax notices the Sevora has clenched his claws.

"There are not enough pilots," Avan says. "The war has decimated our numbers. Whereas you can simply train another Flaum, we must first have a Sevora ready to take a host. Then, only after the Sevora has established control, can we begin training."

Avan leads them to a larger shuttle, an ovoid craft with no visible cannons on the outside. No weapons at all, in fact. Its sleek exterior, painted in the greens and whites of a peaceful ship, confirms the craft's purpose. That it sits ready, with a a set of four armed Flaum soldiers at the foot of the shuttle's metal legs tells Sax that their arrival here isn't unexpected.

Perhaps Avan would be making this trip even if Sax and the others hadn't gone along.

The shuttle loads through an elevator, rather than a more usual ramp. The platform sinks down from the middle of the shuttle on four thin poles which set themselves on the ground. The craft has three struts; one in front and two thick legs at the aft, and its engines point towards the bay door. Avan singles out Bas and Lan with his claws and tells them to get on the platform, which is too small to hold all of them at once. Bas catches Sax's eye, and he blinks twice at her. Affirmative.

They will go along with Avan's plan. For now.

A pair of Flaum, each holding a primed, heavy miner nearly as large as themselves, join Bas and Lan on the platform. Sax knows these weapons—a trigger, a big battery pack, and a wide nozzle. Capable of blasting hot energy in close quarters and guaranteed not to miss anything in front of you. If Bas or Lan want to attack, they'll have to kill or disarm the Flaum immediately, or be melted into char.

Once they settle, the platform shoots up into the belly of the shuttle with the whistling shunt of hydraulics. Moments later it descends again, empty. Avan waves Gar on, and two other Flaum join him. Sax starts to board the platform, but Avan holds up a claw. "Not yet. I need to make sure your friends won't get any ideas. Tear apart my soldiers and leave me down here."

Sax would have made the same choice had he been in Avan's place. The four Oratus, left alone with the Flaum, might have gone for an attack like that. Commandeer the shuttle. Though, Sax thinks, it would have been a short hijacking. Without a way to open the docking bay doors, Avan could have had other guards blow up the shuttle where it sits.

Which means Avan has a different reason for keeping Sax down here.

"Why now?" Sax hisses, turning to Avan. "We have the clear advantage. There is no reason for us to meet with you. To save your species."

"Sax, your friends would see me dead in a moment. That one, Gar, is particularly violent. You do not seem quite so bloodthirsty. Why is that?"

"I am disgusted by you," Sax answers as the shuttle's platform descends again, empty. "But you are not the objective. We won't risk our mission for one Sevora."

"Then, perhaps, you can see what so many of your species cannot. What I hope your commanders will be able to understand."

"And that is?"

"A vital piece of information," Avan says. "One that the Sevora learned by accident. From an unexpected host. Knowledge that, if broadcast widely, would be dismissed as slander. Propaganda. But if allowed to grow quietly, it could change everything. Reset the galaxy, and our places in it."

"A bold statement, Sevora." Sax follows Avan onto the platform. "Given your imminent defeat, I'd think you would say anything to save yourself."

"I thought the same when I heard it," Avan replies as the platform rises. "Even in our dire need, we aren't ones to leap at false hopes. Except, Sax, I now believe it is true. The Sevora have sought confirmation, and have found enough evidence to make our claim more likely than not. And if it is true, Sax, then all of our species would be fools not to act on it."

The inside of the shuttle is a luxury that Sax has never known: lounging couches, with straps for any sort of acceleration, splay around a wide area bordered with shifting works of art. Images from other worlds, vistas of orange mountains and green oceans, captivate the other Oratus.

Their Flaum guards seem similarly fascinated, the miners hanging loose at their sides. Whatever this ship's purpose today, at one point it had served as the finest pleasure currency could buy.

"A jewel," Avan says of the shuttle as they rise into it. "Designed for different times, but now called to a mission far more important than its original owners ever envisioned."

As Sax looks around the shuttle, he feels the engines begin to rumble. The vibration churns through the ship, and everyone finds their seats. Sax winds up on the end, with Avan conspicuously choosing a spot next to him. Sitting on cushions like these, with a tail, requires contorting his body, and Sax winds his tail around his own waist to keep from sitting on it. The other Oratus do the same, though Avan's tail leaks out to his side, flopping off the edge of the couch towards the floor.

"Will you tell me what this is? The great secret you claim to have?" Sax asks Avan.

"So that you might dispatch me and deliver it yourself?" Avan gives Sax a toothy grin. "I won't take that chance. The words come from me, or from no one."

"If this was your plan, then," Bas says from across the ship. "Why try to kill us?"

"You aren't necessary," Avan replies. "I would be on this ship, heading out into the battle, with or without you. If I can save our seed ship from your claws, and help my own goals in the process, then why not do so?"

As Avan speaks, the shuttle lifts and burns out of the docking bay. Sax looks out the front window, into the laser show of the fight still underway. The four of them left the middle of the seed ship to find a way into the very heart, and now they have it.

Avan's promises are intriguing, of course, so Sax will see to it that Avan will make it to Evva, but Sax also has a mission. One he will not fail.

Jakkan waits for me at Damantum's gates. The Emperor has assembled a vast train there, with soldiers standing in rows along with porters to carry goods. The Emperor is there as well, standing on his own chariot, to which are hitched a pair of large creatures. They're called, so I'm told by one of the guards, oxen. Bulky beasts with horns, most are used for field duty, which is why I haven't seen them throughout the city.

These two, though, sport mantles of blue and gold washing down from their massive horns, across their backs and spilling into tassels down their sides. The Emperor's chariot is opulence. Thankfully it's a cloudy day, or I'm not sure I could stand all the flashing gold and gems.

My spot, so I'm told, is walking next to the chariot. A place of honor, and as nobody else in the force—save Viera—is riding, I don't begrudge the opportunity.

We're leaving with a purpose: to convince the Lunare that a fight with the Charre will be costly, will be terrible, and is not condoned by either their god or ours. To that end, I see a series of woven crates supported with bamboo poles stretched across the backs of Charre workers. I open one to confirm my suspicions—

inside are some of the weapons we've been making, waiting for their chance.

Crude, but the overall design should work. I would not be the one to pull the trigger, Kaishi. Let someone else see if it explodes.

I have no intention of fighting the Lunare. I'm not here for a battle, and, after the Pits, have no desire to start one.

"I have a gift for you," Jakkan says as we say goodbyes near the front gates. I wait, but he doesn't present anything. "Your spot. In the train. I've elected to stay behind in the city and give you my place at the Emperor's side."

"I don't understand?"

"I'm giving you the chance to supplant me." Jakkan spreads a warm smile. "I've seen it. During these last few days especially. You are truly one with Ignos, and you deserve your place at the Emperor's right hand. I will stay away to watch the two of you grow a great empire and will serve you as best I can. Right now that means taking care of our city and carrying on the work that you started. Destroy the Lunare, Kaishi, and bolster the Charre with their bones."

"Destroy?" I haven't heard Jakkan use such harsh language, but there's anger in those words. Pride too. "I think we're going to negotiate. To convince them to leave us alone."

Jakkan laughs. "With the Lunare? The Emperor is bringing you on this journey for a reason, Kaishi. To see that no civilization, no upstarts from the mountains, dare provoke us. They will either run, or the Emperor will see them crushed."

I'm stunned by the admission and can't think of anything to say. My expression only delights Jakkan further, and he leaves me then, staring after him as he gathers followers to wave at our march from the gates.

Come now. You can't really be surprised? What is the point of power if not to destroy your enemies and raise up your allies?

I've driven a knife through flesh and bone. My words have brought about at least one death. My hands are not clean. But those were my choices, and I knew the consequences. If Jakkan is right, then what I've been helping the Charre make will result in conquest, in fire and death.

Either you or them, Kaishi. Do not be so naive. Think of how far you've come.

I do, and feel like retching.

When the horns sound to march, I'm alongside the right ox and one of its large, brown eyes stares back at me. It's in shadow as the Ignos' morning light hits the other side of the beast's long head, and in its iris I see a warped reflection of myself. I'm wearing my finery; the green headdress and bright cape, my mosswrap is back at the Vaos, not fit for a high priestess.

I don't know who I'm looking at.

"You seem distracted," The Emperor, above me in his chariot and adorned in all sorts of glittering, blue and gold robes, says. "Are you not honored to be on this great and glorious march?"

"I've never marched with an Emperor before. It's overwhelming." I say something to say something.

The Emperor chuckles, then raises his right hand. At the signal, horns blow again and the column begins to march. Thousands of warriors with all manner of skins on their shoulders. Servants, porters, cooks and caretakers mix in. For the first time I feel what it is like to move with an army, to be a part of something so large and in motion. The thunder and rhythm.

It almost lets me forget what Jakkan said.

Almost.

After an hour without conversation, the Emperor turns back to Damantum and I follow his gaze, careful to keep my march steady. The walls stand tall. People are on top of them, still waving at the departing army's snake. "All of them believe in us, Kaishi. It can be hard to leave under the weight of so many expectations, but you will get use to it. Our mission demands it. Ignos demands it."

"Jakkan says you want to kill them." I can't keep from asking anymore. "The Lunare?"

"As they wish to own us," the Emperor replies. "I am the chosen one. There can be no other ruler. The Lunare proclaim themselves the divine people. How can I allow such a thing? How can my people keep their faith when such blasphemies stand?"

"So death is the only way?"

"If the rumors are true, the Lunare leader will offer another path to us, only to stab us in the back should we choose to walk it." The Emperor shakes his head. "They conquer through lies as well as force. Any negotiation will end in blood, one way or another."

After the rest of the morning bleeds away with footsteps, the troops at the front announce a halt. Other, friendly forces are coming. The new warriors resolve themselves into Malo and his band, returning from Damantum's outer villages, and coming back with foul news.

"They're falling before the Lunare," Malo explains to the Emperor while I listen. "Some try to fight, but give in when the Lunare spit their fire. Others don't even bother. They bow and scrape. Trade freedom for their lives. Embrace Lunare's rule, and march with them."

After the briefing, I excuse myself from the Emperor's company and find Malo back with Viera, near the rear of the column and being pulled along on a small cart. Malo greets me with a soft smile. "So you found her."

"She lives," I say, and seeing the two of them together brings unexpected heat. "With no help from you."

Malo nods. "The woman is an enemy. She deserves what came to her."

"She promised to save me. Just as you did."

Malo hesitates, then reaches into his belt, unhooks Viera's weapon. Places it on the cart next to the Lunare.

"I hope she still can." Malo leaves before I can say another word, vanishing back into the press of troops.

That one is moody. Though I think he still means you well.

There are thousands of people here. I believe I can count on two of them, and one of those is still lying in a cart, eyes closed and broken.

When the horns blow to resume the march, I leave Viera's side and head back to the front.

"Tonight," the Emperor says when I've rejoined my place. "You will demonstrate your miracles. Make sure they work as Ignos demands. When we meet the Lunare, there will be no room for failure."

The movements need to be precise. Use every moment. Sax seeks out their eyes.

The shuttle coasts free of the seed ship, and as the craft leaves the sliding plates and their magnetic field behind, it lurches. The Flaum, sitting on the couches, jostle from side to side. Their hands leave the hafts of their miners to steady themselves. Sax sees Avan notice. Sees Avan's mouth open, his warning shout begin.

Too late.

Across the shuttle, Bas strikes at the Flaum on both sides of her. Two claws on her left, two claws on her right, each with three sharp razors raking at their targets. Going for the miners, for the hands reaching towards them. Lan and Gar do the same, as does Sax. A simple grab, clench, and tear. Now without arms of their own, the Flaum freeze in shock.

"What are you doing?" Avan finally finishes his exclamation.

The Sevora tries to rise, but unlike Sax and the others, whose tails don't interfere with their legs, Avan's inexperience makes the action difficult. Unwieldy in the low gravity.

Sax springs towards the shuttle's ceiling, catches himself on the inside hull with his claws, then launches back down at Avan. As the captured Oratus makes it to his feet, Sax slams into him, knocking the creature to the ground. Each of Sax's claws pins one of Avan's, while Sax's tail goes over his shoulder and wraps itself around Avan's throat.

"Do not struggle," Sax says. "The shuttle is ours. You have no reason to die for it."

Though Sax keeps his eyes on Avan, he can hear the sounds from the cockpit. Panicked squeaks from the Flaum, and the subsequent orders from Lan to turn the shuttle up and around. Orders Lan finishes with a simple statement: if the Flaum and the Sevora in their heads obey, then Lan and Gar won't tear them all to pieces where they sit.

Bas joins Sax, holding a pair of the heavy miners in her arms and pointing them down at Avan.

"Why haven't you finished him?" Bas asks. "He is an abomination."

Sax tightens his tail around Avan's throat to keep the Sevora from getting any ideas, and looks at his pair. "He states that he has valuable information that could change the course of the war. I can't take the chance that he is not lying."

"We cannot take him with us. He won't sit quietly while we destroy the ship."

"No. Which is why Gar and Lan will take him to Evva. She'll decide whether his information is worth his life." Sax turns back to Avan. "I offer you this, Sevora. A journey to our side. A chance to tell your tale. Will you accept?"

"That is what we were doing, before you murdered my crew," Avan says once Sax loosens his tail enough so the Sevora can speak.

"And that is what you will continue to do. Bas, ready one of the evac mods. We'll use that."

Bas hisses her dissent. "Reckless, Sax. We can guide the shuttle in. Its size alone guarantees damage to the seed ship's core."

Avan's eyes flick between them, wide, red, and shivering. Sax ignores him, "You heard me, Bas. Until the mission ends, I make the call. Ready the mod."

"What are you trying to do?" Avan asks, but Sax doesn't respond.

He watches Bas for a moment, making sure she actually goes to the evacuation module's door and begins punching in the commands to ready the craft. Bas does what Sax asks, though Sax knows he'll catch many mouthfuls about it later.

If there is a later.

"Gar, Lan," Sax announces. "You will fly the shuttle back to Evva. Make sure Avan gets a chance to tell his promised story. If it fails to justify his existence, I trust you will rend the skin from his bones. Now, you will bring the shuttle across the center of the seed ship. Bas and I will use the evac mod to make our assault."

The two Oratus greet the command with silence. Sax refuses to turn his head away from Avan—the body of an Oratus is a weapon, and Sax dares not let it out of his sight.

"We will honor your command, Sax, even if we don't understand it," Lan finally says.

"You see, Sevora?" Sax hisses after Lan speaks. "We are loyal without control. Without giving up our bodies to your parasites."

"I am trying to save my species." Avan, for the first time, sounds broken.

"Until you convince me otherwise," Sax says. "It is my goal to destroy it."

Gar approaches then, trading watch on the pilots with Lan, and places a clawed hand on Sax's shoulder. Without speaking, the two exchange positions, with Gar holding Avan against the ground and wrapping his own tail around the Sevora's neck. Only when Sax stands and heads towards the evac mod, does Gar say anything, "You are taking my blood, brother."

"I shall spill enough for both of us, brother," Sax replies, as custom demands. The answer satisfies Gar, who focuses on his prisoner. Sax knows the Oratus won't move from that position until something blows him away or they land on the Vincere ship.

"The launch window is approaching," Lan announces from the cockpit. "Get ready."

Bas waits inside the cramped evac mod, the benches inside too small for her body. Sax joins her, squeezing into the opposite side. Their tails meet in the middle, looping around each other. Without any sign, any words or glances, Sax puts his claws out and Bas clasps them with her own. She accepts his apology, forgives the harsh words, and they promise to fight together through whatever is coming, all with a touch.

So it is with one's pair.

The evac mod has no windows. Shielded with thick metal to block both the heat from an atmosphere, radiation from outside space, and the inevitable impact a jettison from a crashing ship would cause, the evac mod serves a singular purpose: to get its passengers to their destination alive.

So when Sax shuts the door behind him with a simple press of the two-button control panel, the two of them wait for Lan to get the shuttle in the right position without worry.

They will have one shot at this. A speeding projectile aiming directly at the heart of the seed ship. Miss, and they will either crash elsewhere and be stuck in the same plight as before, or they could burn through the ship entirely and fall into the crushing gravity of the giant orange planet.

A shunt sounds. A moving of metal. The brief wail of an alarm.

No other clue announces the evac mod leaving the shuttle. No other sensations bleed through to the two Oratus that they are now in motion.

They fly in silence.

That night, as an endless number of campfires illuminate the desert around us, I gather with a group of Charre warriors, including Malo, to run a final test on what the Cache has given us.

Four woven boxes are arrayed in a half circle on the edge of the army camp, with nothing but sand on the other side. Nomis' light shimmers from above, mixing with the flickering orange to cast our shadows out beyond.

As the warriors watch, I go to the first crate and open its lid. Inside appear to be blades. The same black-glass that marks the sacrificial knives. Only these blades are loosely connected. A single long central fiber runs between them, flexible and twisting. It ends in a sturdy grip of wound rope, with a soft bulge on the underside. I take hold of it, and lift it out. It's long; almost twice my height, and the weapon coils around my feet. Despite the sharp blades, the device is light. Easy to hold.

"This is called a shard," I say, remembering the name from what the Cache told me. "You can whip it at your enemies, like this."

I heft the shard and snap it forward, cutting back with my hand at the last instant to crack the blades. They slash forward, biting through the air and clashing against each other, throwing sparks. Vicious, but not all that different from the kukri they hold already.

Until I use the trick.

I twist my wrist so everyone can see the small orb attached to the end of the shard's grip. "Here, however, is the secret. Squeeze this. A little bit of oil will leak down through the fiber and onto the glass blades. Then all you need to do is crack it again."

I do what I say. Squeeze the pump and sheen coats the rope's fibers. I crack the shard again. Sparks fly as the black-glass clacks. Only this time the sparks catch fire. Soon the entire rope, except the handle, is aflame.

"See how it burns, but the fiber beneath does not?" I say. "You can strike fear into their hearts. Over and over again."

I let the whip settle into the sand, the dirt snuffing out the remnants of the fire. The expressions on the warriors' faces are suitably impressed, though they're not amazed yet. An interesting weapon, but hardly a divine miracle.

I'm just getting started.

From the next crate, I pull out something very similar to Viera's pistol. A wooden stock in a metal frame.

"The Lunare will load a black powder into their weapons before they fire. This will give us an opportunity. Whether to strike with our hands, or with these," I lift the weapon, aim into the distance, and pull the trigger.

With a pop, the gun makes a loud noise. My shoulder rocks back, but I ignore the bruising, the brief bite of pain as the weapon kicks into me. No time for that now. "Rather than packing the powder into the weapon, we pack it into the ammunition. Press the trigger, you strike the shot and it explodes forward. Each of these can hold twelve at a time."

What I don't say is that the entire Charre army only has three of the guns. Their point, after all, is not to decimate an army but to show that a fight would be fruitless. Too costly for either side. At least, that's what I hope.

The third crate contains more miracles. Globes that, when tossed, explode into tremendous gouts of flaming fire and noise. Others that don't burn but spread noxious gas, causing people near them to descend into coughing fits and crying agony.

The very last crate holds not implements of war, but the stuff of peace. Ointments and salves. Medical tools that can repair even the most grievous of injuries. I want these for the Charre, yes, but also as a potential peace offering. A chance not to kill, but to bring two peoples together over mutual benefit.

I'm thinking too of my own tribe. How destroyed they would be if the Charre and Lunare made the jungle their battleground. How much better everything would be, instead, if the two factions made my old village a center of trade. Of peace.

Malo comes up after the demonstration, as the other warriors leave, chattering amongst themselves in excited voices. For once, he doesn't look at me like I'm something to be taken care of. I see the same level stare he gives to Jakkan and other warriors.

Respect.

"I never believed, when I took you from your village, that this would be the result," Malo says. "I thought, at best, you were a talented girl. That you had some inspiring prayers. Not that you would reshape our entire empire."

"I thought the same thing, but Ignos knew better. He's used me."

"For the good of the Charre. The good of our people."

"Your people," I reply. "One reason I'm still here is because I know the Lunare will be worse for us. If I succeed, perhaps the Emperor will spare my people your brutality."

"You've become so hostile." Malo's face is curious, intent, concerned. "Why? What have I done?"

"It's more what you didn't do," I say. "You didn't warn me. You didn't guide me through Damantum, but threw me at Jakkan's feet and left. You did not tell me about the Pits. You claimed to support me, to believe me, but you tore me from my family and left me to live or die on my own. Should I be grateful to you for that?"

Malo takes a moment, stares at the campfires. "I didn't know what to do. I'm a warrior, not some father figure. Not a guide."

"It doesn't matter what you are. You shouldn't have to be trained to know when someone you call a friend needs help."

Malo says nothing. After a minute, with me waiting every second of it, the warrior mutters a goodbye and stomps off.

I go back to Viera, only to find that the two priests caring for her are ecstatic. Or at least, as happy as Charre priests can get.

"High priestess," one of them exclaims as I near. "Her fever is broken. The treatments, they seem to have worked. The infection subsided."

I push past the priest and kneel by Viera. Place my hand on her forehead. She does feel cooler. The red around her scars has faded to a more pasty pale, but the Lunare's eyes remain closed. She breathes lightly. Yes, she might live, but Viera is not healthy yet.

Not that I have time to worry. Tomorrow, according to the scouts, we meet the Lunare.

The impact comes in a shuddering crash. No lead-in. No warning sign. Just one second floating with a slight sensation of rapid movement, and in the next the evac mod bounces Sax into Bas. The mod crackles and rolls, the sound of rending metal making it to Sax not as noise but as vibrations. He feels the wreckage in his bones.

The small lights in the mod go out. Plunge the container, which has no windows, into black. Then a flaring red. A warning.

"You have a mask still," Sax says to Bas, who confirms it. "You can go."

"The vacuum will kill you."

"The mission takes precedence." Bas reaches out, runs a claw down the side of Sax's long, narrow face, "Patience, dear one. The ship will take care of us."

A risk. Most ships of any size have measures in place to keep a hull tear from destroying everything. Some could deploy electromagnetic shields across gaps, using pressure and magnetism to keep everything inside the ship from rushing out. Others use temporary sprays; sealants launched from repair robots to close a hole until more permanent measures could be used.

Bas would be hoping for one of those. The danger, of course, is that something else could find their evac mod in the meantime. Set up an ambush and blow the two of them away the moment they open the door.

"It's not worth the risk." Sax brushes Bas' claw.

"Tell me, Sax, would you not do the same for me?"

Sax opens his mouth to say that he would carry on with the mission. That he would put success above any one person. But no words come out. He seems unable to form the sentence. Bas hisses in laughter at the sight of it.

"A pairing is more than a single mission," Bas whispers. "You, Sax, are worth more alive to me than a thousand seed ships."

Sax adjusts his tail so he can sit back against the wall of the evac mod. Stares at Bas. Reaches out with his claws again and clasps hers. They might be trapped, but Sax will make the most of these moments.

"When did you know?" Sax says. "When did you know you cared about me?"

"From the moment I saw what lay behind the danger in those eyes of yours."

"What do you mean?"

Bas tilts her head to one side, "Most Oratus are weapons, Sax. They live and breathe violence. It's what we're taught to love. I do. You do. But we don't stop there, do we?"

"You're talking about Avan."

"I'm talking about many moments, Sax, when we chose a different path. When I noticed you could see other ways, that's when I knew you were the one I wanted. The one I needed."

Before Sax can reply, the lights in the evac mod flip from red to a deep blue. Pressure and oxygen. What vacuum had existed after the crash had been fixed by someone or something. They can leave.

"We'll come back to this, Bas." Sax reaches for the control panel that opens the door. "I wouldn't mind hearing more about how amazing I am."

Bas doesn't laugh. Instead she yanks Sax's arm away from the panel. "I go first," Bas says, pushing Sax, gently, towards the back of the evac mod. "I'm the one with the mask, remember?"

When the evac mod's door swings open, it reveals a sparking mess of wires, torn metal sheeting that had been a ceiling or floor, and flickering white lights. Bas pokes her head out, then withdraws back into the capsule.

"We're in a rounded area," Bas says. "Hanging at the top of it. There's a chamber directly below us. Can't see into it. This room rings it. Appears to be food, oxygen, and water, at least, piped in here from elsewhere on the ship."

"It's a sealed bridge," Sax says. Not unusual on massive ships or ones carrying precious cargo. Keep the captain and controls separate from the passengers to reduce the odds of a hijacking or, as in this case, attackers from reaching the place where they could control everything else.

"And we're inside it." Bas flashes Sax a toothy grin, then scrambles out of the mod and drops. Sax follows, drifting towards the floor. From outside the mod, Sax can see the circular section, as high as the other parts of the seed ship they've visited. In the middle, directly below their hanging mod, is a wide cylinder that almost reaches up to them.

The structure lacks windows and, in the white light cast from globed bulbs scattered along the ring's walls, seems entirely black. At ground level, the section appears to have a variety of amenities: Tubes opening to bins for water, counters for food, and one large waste pit that, Sax figures, would lead back to the seed ship's recycler.

Someone could live here indefinitely.

Sax hits the floor and balances on his legs, letting his claws dig small grooves into the metal. Something tickles his vents. A smell that doesn't belong in a place like this. Too much carbon in the air. As though he's stuck in a room with a bunch of hard-breathing Flaum.

"Do you smell that?" Sax asks Bas, who's loping around the central cylinder, looking for a door.

"Faulty electronics?" Bas replies as she moves, and Sax begins to circle the opposite way. The cylinder building isn't so large that they would run out of earshot. "From the crash?"

"Too natural." Sax goes around, but there doesn't seem to be any clear door. No lock, no sliding gateway. It's clear, though, that the command cluster they're looking for sits inside those walls. "Can we break through?"

Bas doesn't hesitate. She swipes a claw across the metal, sounding a shriek through the space. Her claws leave a silver line, but no tear.

They won't be getting in that way.

"Whomever is in there has to leave some time," Bas says, glancing at the food and drink receptacles. "We can wait for them."

Sax is about to answer, but the carbon smell smogs the air. Blots out every other scent. He focuses on it. Opens his vents and inhales. His body tells him the scent is stronger form above. Sax looks, and freezes.

A large shadow moves on the ceiling.

"Bas, we're not alone," Sax says, as the darkness falls towards them.

We only march for an hour the next day, and stop well before Ignos reaches its zenith, in a valley with Tutio behind us at one end and the sandy waste leading to my jungle on the other. The Emperor proclaims that the Lunare will come to us, and not the other way around, so we wait.

I try to make use of the time. Viera is still out, so once the column stops moving, I help the priests set her up towards the back of the forces. Then I work with the miracles, positioning the crates near the Emperor and making sure that the warriors who would open, who would show off their contents, understand how to use them.

The Emperor himself still has the small pistol made just for him. He holds it in his right hand, while in his left he carries a ceremonial scepter topped with a golden depiction of Ignos, each of its six rays sporting rubies, diamonds, and sapphires. It's glorious and majestic and I'm entirely happy to let the Emperor take the spotlight.

War, I'm learning, isn't my favorite thing. Too much grit, too many orders, and the constant expectation of death hang over everything.

Around noon, dust appears on the horizon, growing closer as it sweeps into the valley in front of the volcano. The same brown cloud that I saw around the Solare tribesmen. This one grows faster, moves more quickly towards us. The ground tremors with the pounding of feet and larger things. Monsters I've never seen before.

The Lunare, astride their rolling, wooden and rock constructs in the center, are surrounded far and wide by the stamping march of other tribes. I can't look away from the Lunare... buildings. I don't know what else to call them. They look like boats, with a curved front prow, yet have turning wheels propelling them along the ground.

Large white, scaled beasts with no eyes and many legs pull the things towards us, grappled to their tasks by thick iron chains linked to collars.

All too clear, as well, are the openings in the sides of the hulls where gray tubes poke out, pointing in our direction.

Fassoth. How are they here?

I don't understand what Ignos is asking about, and he quickly moves on. Tells me that it's important to avoid those creatures, as they're deadly when angered. Then he falls silent, as Ignos is prone to do.

"Look at how many there are," I say to the Emperor. "We're outnumbered."

"I did not bring all of the Charre with us for a reason," The Emperor says, sounding as unconcerned as he looks. "What will decide this conflict is not strength in numbers. They will not take Damantum, or eliminate my people with their weapons. They will take it by destroying our faith. The Charre will fall when they stop believing in me. In Ignos.

"How much of the force you see before you are Lunare? Not many. The cowards from the mountains hide in their toys. They rule by fear. When we show the tribes they have collected that the Lunare are nothing to be scared of, they will turn to our side."

Don't stay near him.

I don't understand Ignos's sudden warning.

The history of all things is splattered with the blood of heroes who led from the front of their forces. The Emperor, astride that chariot, makes a grand target of himself. You, next to him, are as likely to get hit by a stray shot.

"How will you be safe?" I ask the Emperor.

"Ignos will protect me. Even these tribesmen, who call the Lunare their leader, even they will turn against these invaders if they strike me down outright. The Lunare will know this."

Malo joins us as we watch the Lunare approach. Their boats stand three times as tall as the Emperor. There are three of them, each with a pair of the white, furred beasts, and they rise above the Charre forces.

I guess there are several hundred Lunare packed on and around the boats. Around those, however, are thousands of tribesmen. Gathered from the jungles and desert lands, forced or coerced into marching with these strange things.

It's not the war Father envisioned being the end of the Solare—the bows and arrows and spears in the jungle trees, but instead a facing off between forces armed with weapons he could never have imagined.

A Lunare steps to the fore of the center boat. Unlike the Emperor, he isn't clad in golden finery. He doesn't wear a cape or carry a staff. His face is smudged with dirt, which makes his silver helmet, shaped in a way that makes me think of mushroom caps, gleam. His uniform is simple cloth, and there is nothing about what he wears that speaks of leadership, except his stance. His tall standing, broad gaze, and the sheer respect with which all of the other Lunare direct him as the man levels his stare at the Emperor.

Silence fills the expectant air.

The Emperor taps his staff on his chariot's floor, and the oxen lope forward a pace, until they are nose to nose with the creatures Ignos calls Fassoths. He looks up at the Lunare leader.

"Should I go?" I whisper to Malo, beside me now, who shakes his head.

"The Emperor must be the absolute authority, high priestess."

I hear the honorific. Malo has called me priestess before, but always with a twist of kindness, like a friend. Now it comes with a harsh formality. Maybe I'd been too hard on him. Too difficult.

Remember what I said before. Now is not the time to concern yourself with his feelings. Instead, win this confrontation. Claim your mantle.

And then what? Ignos keeps pushing me towards more and greater things, but to what end? How much would I lose along the way?

End? This won't ever end Kaishi. We'll keep going and growing. First the Charre, then all of the tribes, and further and beyond until you'll have gone farther than you could imagine.

What if I don't want to?

Ignos doesn't answer, and my momentary reverie shatters as the Emperor raises his staff. The warriors bearing the miracles step forward. First, comes the one with the shard. He squeezes the handle and cracks the black glass against each other. Starts a swirling fire.

I hear the gasps around me, but the Lunare seem unimpressed. Two other Charre come forward, holding the rapid-fire guns. They aim up, over the heads of the Lunare, and fire two quick shots apiece.

Again there are gasps. This time, I notice the Lunare paying attention; eyes drawn to the guns.

"We have many more," the Emperor shouts. "Ignos gives us his vision and we manifest it."

The Emperor's words seem to move the tribes. The Solare and tribal men on the sides of the Lunare shift, glance at each other and up at their new leaders, who in turn look to their man in the center for a counter. My heart twists at the strange smile that comes over his face. If the Lunare leader has any doubts, fears or worries, I can't see any.

"A grand show for one who has so little. We come here not to see your playthings, Emperor, but to prove that there is a better life. That the Lunare bring paradise and providence. All of these tribes here know of what we speak. All that remains is for you to learn." The leader, then, runs his eyes over the front of the Charre army.

He stops on me.

"One woman among your troops, Emperor?" the Lunare leader cries. "And without a weapon?"

"A high priestess is necessary for Ignos to bless our journey," the Emperor replies.

"Bless? So you say *she* carries Ignos' words?" the Lunare crows.

Malo wraps his hand around my arm. "Be ready," he whispers.

"Ready for what?" I whisper back.

It's not like I can do anything, standing there with a thousand troops at my back and a host of enemies in front of me.

"Through her, Ignos tell us your days in this land are over. That, to save the lives of you and your men, you should return to your mountains. Crawl back to your holes in the ground." The Emperor booms his voice now, and I understand they're talking more to the armies than to each other.

The Lunare reaches into his belt, pulls a pistol free, and points it at me. "Surely, if this high priestess has the protection of your god, I would not be able to kill her?"

"You have seen the gifts Ignos has given us." The Emperor makes no move to attack, no move to shift soldiers in front of me. "Is that not evidence enough?"

"Tricks," the Lunare announces. "Lies meant to twist your minds. Again I ask you, if I shoot this girl, will Ignos protect her?"

"He will find a way," the Emperor replies.

The Lunare nods. Keeps his finger on the trigger. Then swings the weapon towards the Emperor, and fires. The gunshot cracks loud; in that instant it's the only noise in the entire universe.

I don't see the bullet, but I do see the smoke. The Emperor slumps forward against the front of his chariot, and the oxen, frightened, turn to run. They trample away, rumbling down the line between the armies, the Emperor's body tumbles from the chariot into the dirt before me.

"Do you see? His god has failed him. Your true Emperor stands before you now. Follow me, and lead your fellows into the light." The Lunare raises his pistol high and waves it.

I stare with Malo and all the others. Aghast. How can the Emperor, the holy one, die like this?

The fight hasn't started, and the Lunare have already won.

Sax figures his instincts, those twitchy actions that come without conscious thought, are the main reason he's survived this long. They save his life again when his tail, along with Sax's legs, pushes him into a roll along the ground. Behind him, the creature dives out of the shadows.

Bas rolls the opposite way, so that when the two Oratus stand, the creature is directly between them. Which, considering it's a Fassoth, is less than optimal. The Fassoth is a nightmare to look at: its long, ridged, snow-scaled body bleeds into eight trunk-like legs, each ending with a splayed assortment of claws. Its head is a hard bulb, eye- and earless. White hair puffs out between the scales, thin and light. On their icy home world, the Fassoth hunt by crouching down, waiting for something to pass. Hiding in the drifts.

Most of the time, Fassoths serve in labor capacities. Strong and nigh tireless, so long as they're kept fed, Sax has found plenty of them on Sevora worlds, has fought more than his fair share. Never, though, in tight confines like this. Never with only a single partner, unarmed. Still, if there's one guide to fighting a Fassoth, it's to keep moving.

So Sax goes. Takes a leap towards the creature's back. As Sax flies, though, the Fassoth twists, those hairs picking up the shifts in the air. It rolls as Sax soars overhead, gravity now acting as an impediment and keeping Sax in the air long enough so that, instead of striking the Fassoth's back with claws extended, Sax bombs directly into the creature's clawed legs.

Where the Fassoth's true terror waits. On the ends of each of those legs, in the center of the claws, sits a gnashing maw of sandy teeth. Rock-molded and gummed over time to form jagged edges. Sax is about to get caught by these things. Grabbed and chewed to pieces.

Until Bas, streaking through the air in the opposite direction, tackles Sax and pushes both of them back to the ground away from the Fassoth. Sax taps her with a claw in thanks. They separate, crouch and hold ready. The Fassoth squirms back onto its feet and shifts towards them. Sax sees the creature's rocky plates flex, pushing air in and out. Not too unlike his vents. Those are the Fassoth's weak spots. If he can get his claws between its armor, he'll be able to tear the Fassoth to pieces.

"I'll distract, you go for the back," Sax hisses.

"Flip it," Bas replies. "I still have my mask."

"That won't help against this."

"Stop talking and attack," Bas says as she charges the Fassoth. The creature, more than three times her size, takes the bait and runs towards her, all eight of its legs shoving along the ground.

Sax, again, goes for the air. This time jumping against the side wall of the ring and using his claws to dig in, to catch himself above the ground. Sax sits still for a moment. If he doesn't move, the Fassoth will have a hard time knowing where he is. Will forget about him and focus on Bas, who, using her tail and widespread arms, darts back and forth. Creates as many moving molecules as possible. With so much motion, the Fassoth will have to guess where she is.

Bas begins to back up as the Fassoth slinks closer. When it thinks she's near, the Fassoth rises up on its four back legs, using its front four to swipe at Bas. She ducks and weaves, ignoring openings in favor of keeping herself alive. A pair of the Fassoth's limbs come in high, followed by its second two sweeping low. Bas, using gravity, twists through a flip in the air, the giant legs gliding just over and under her. Sax would marvel at the move, but his own time has arrived.

Normally, from here, Sax would open up with miners. Spray concentrated beams of energy to bisect the Fassoth, or shave off its legs and leave it incapacitated. Sax has no miners. Sax is unarmed, save for his claws.

They'll have to be enough.

Pressing off the back wall, Sax launches himself at the Fassoth. His angle comes in shallow, so that when he nears, and the creature begins to turn towards him, Sax twists and reaches with his claws. They slide across the Fassoth's back, feeling their way between the slats and digging into softer tissue. The pull turns Sax the rest of the way around as he crosses the Fassoth's body, and the Oratus plants his legs on the Fassoth's side, digging his claws in as the creature, having rotated the wrong way, begins turning back.

Sax presses off again, jumping away from the Fassoth towards the central building's wall. The move should have brought the Fassoth's attention back to Bas, who is trying to dance in, swiping at the legs. Fassoths aren't intelligent. It should obey its instincts. Go after the closer target. But this one doesn't. This one ignores Bas and spins to follow Sax. As Sax lands against the building, the Fassoth rushes him. Those legs propel the creature too fast for Sax to jump away.

So Sax doesn't. He hears Bas try a desperate roar, one the Fassoth ignores. Sax lets his claws slip from the wall and wraps himself in his arms, his tail, and prepares to be crushed.

The Fassoth barrels into Sax, smashes the Oratus into the building. Sax feels the Fassoth's sharp claws on the ends of its legs bite into him. The teeth cut Sax's skin. But the thing about low gravity is that it's hard to stop yourself once you get moving, and a Fassoth can get moving like few other creatures in the galaxy. It smashes into the central cylinder, its bulk carrying into the wall and pressing against it.

Sax figures the side walls are designed to stop lasers. To protect against cutting weapons and beams. The top and bottom of the structure, the most likely targets for a ramming like Sax and Bas had attempted with the evac mod, might be reinforced against a crash. The sides, though? Where would a heavy impact come from in a tight space?

The wall bends, twists and breaks as the Fassoth crushes through.

The impact flattens those trunk legs against Sax, crushing the Oratus into the Fassoth's underbelly, and, despite the claws digging into his arms, Sax fights back. He falls into the manic spirit hiding within every Oratus. The bloodlust. Activated, at times, with Stim, here it comes naturally. The stinging pain from the Fassoth's teeth vanishes, replaced by pure, unbroken fury.

Sax cuts, slashes, bites and lashes even as the Fassoth does the same to him. Until, suddenly, the creature whips Sax through the air into the far wall. He slides along the metal to rest on the cold floor.

Across from him, Sax can see the center of the seed ship. With one of its walls destroyed, the rest collapse, the sides folding against each other and bending out across the ring. The Fassoth, with Bas digging into its back, writhes, but Sax has done the damage. Cut deep enough. These are death throes.

His eyes drift to the center, to the leader of the seed ship, the Sevora they had been sent to eliminate.

What he sees makes perfect, horrifying sense.

Panic is quick to turn to anger.

I see the Emperor's body before angry cracks split the air again. Directly behind me. Malo's taken one of the miracles from the Charre warrior. The one that can fire multiple rounds. Malo fires them all.

The shots strike the Lunare leader, still standing on the front of his boat, one after another. The first two tear the glee from the Lunare's face. The third and fourth knock him back into the boat. The rest of Malo's shots fire into the railings, causing the Lunare to dive away in a shower of wood chips.

As if Malo's attack is some hidden signal, pandemonium erupts: people fly everywhere. Charre warriors rush forward to safeguard the body of their fallen Emperor, while others charge into the Lunare ranks. The Fassoth rear up high and batter anyone that comes close with their legs.

The Lunare seem lost without their leader, calling for a retreat. A bass horn, a hollow rock the Lunare use as an instrument, sounds moments later. This triggers some training in the Fassoth, and they immediately wheel away from the fight, dragging the boats with them.

As for the Solare tribes, they don't know what to do. Leaders on both sides are dead. The Charre avoid them, instead focusing on any Lunare not in a boat, and those they pin down. Tie up and take captive.

Staying here is dangerous. You've played your part. Leave.

Ignos makes sense. I'm at the front of the line. If a focused fight breaks out, if the Lunare decide they aren't quite done, I don't belong in the middle. So I take off. Push my way back through the Charre ranks as they press forward, Malo's ringing voice calling for a full attack.

Others join in with Malo's cry, echoing ululations for the destruction of their enemies. The sheer noise overwhelms me as I struggle away, bouncing off of bodies and squeezing by sharp edges until I reach the rear of the force. Near Viera, her cart, and the priests watching over her. They all stare at me. They have no idea yet of what's happened.

"The Emperor is dead." It's the first, the only thing I say.

The priests fall to their knees and begin to pray, and I let them send their quick words to Ignos before continuing. "With his death, the Emperor gave us a chance to strike down the Lunare leader. They are running now. We'll win."

"What is victory with such a loss? Without our Emperor, we have no one." One of the priests stands as he says the words, though he looks at me as though I have an answer.

"I wouldn't say that," the tone sounds foreign. Then I recognize Viera's voice, hoarse and tired as it is. "I'd say you have your leader standing right there."

The Lunare isn't yet sitting up, but her eyes are open, and she's managing a weak grin my way. I would have smiled back, if not for the frowns and hard stares of the rest of the priests.

Those are not the looks of rejection, but calculation, Kaishi. Stay strong, and they will accept you.

Ignos speaks endlessly about my climb to power. That I'll reach a point where I can save my people by leading those who would destroy them. As I look into the faces of the Charre around me, I realize that it's not me they believe in. It's not me that has the power.

The Charre believe Ignos speaks through me. Our god is choosing my body as his vessel.

You are. Be what they believe.

It's what Father did every day for the village. What my mother did every day for me. I can do it for them.

"Right now, our warriors are fighting and dying while we stand here." I turn as I talk, catching all of the priests, the ones who, through their capes and bangles, staffs and tattoos, speak to all that is holy about Charre and Solare people. "Come with me. Back to the front. Together, we can convince the other tribes to join us and push the Lunare away."

There's hesitation, but nobody wants to look like a coward in front of their god. They fall in line behind me, with me, and together we surge back towards the fighting. This time I don't have to push my way through—the warriors move aside for the priests and, with their blessing, for me.

The front itself is a mess. Bodies scatter across the sand and shrubs, Lunare and Charre and Solare all together. The worst of the fighting is over—the Lunare and their boats are in full retreat. The rest of the tribes stare at us, and with the priests giving me a stage of their own making, at me.

"Followers of Ignos," I yell. "You have seen your falsehoods laid to waste. You have heard the lies of the Lunare dispelled by truths. Our mighty Emperor has given himself to save you from their deception. I bid you not to pick up arms against your brothers, but instead to bare them against the true enemy." I point to the cloud of dust, the boats rising above it in the distance. "Chase them from your lands. From your villages. Reclaim what Ignos has given you, and his miracles will be yours."

As if to accentuate this promise, Malo hefts his gun high, so it's clear to everyone just what miracles would be finding their way forth. Just what this new priestess promises in exchange for loyalty. That is enough. One by one the tribes lay down their weapons, and fall to their knees. All of them, one after another, kneel before me.

Until I stand alone in a circle of thousands.

Even with Bas and the writhing Fassoth tangling in the background, Sax can't look away from the mangled mess in front of him. There were rumors, of course, of what happens when a Sevora reaches full maturity. It takes so much time, is considered so risky for the Sevora itself, that few bother to stay in their hosts long enough for the growth to occur. Instead, at the first sign of the change, the creatures retreat back to the birthing pools or other watery environments, killing their hosts in the process, and wait for new bodies to arrive. Sax has seen those remnants plenty of times; on ships, planets, and space stations that he'd snatched back from the parasites.

This host originally, it appears, had been a Flaum. Sax can see enough fur sticking out to discern that much. Otherwise, though, the thing in front of him resembles nothing he has ever seen. Mounds of discolored flesh pile on one another, fungal eruptions building on what had come before. They rise on stalks, taller than Sax himself at full height, out of what had been the Flaum's body. At the tops of these stalks, the domed tops mesh together with one another, forming an irregular canopy. From that canopy hang, in stringy masses, yellow, orange, and red strands that resemble the tentacles Sevora have while in their swimming, parasitic stage.

All of that is bad enough, but what spins the scene for Sax are the open tubes ringing a rectangular platform in the center, on which the Flaum's body lies. Each of the tubes has a small opening, no larger than the palm of Sax's hand. Red strands from the Sevora hang above many of those tubes, and the ends bulge out, as though something is stuck inside them. Because something is, Sax realizes. The bulges are moving. Independently.

Meanwhile, the orange and yellow strands loop and lift above the top of the Sevora, towards a long series of terminals showing everything from views of the battle beyond the ship, to graphs and meters that, Sax assumes, cover the seed ship's systems.

"Sax!" Bas's yell yanks Sax from his haze, and he sees his pair break free from the Fassoth's arms as the great beast collapses to the floor, twitching away its final seconds of life. "Are you alive?"

"For now," Sax tries to shout the reply, but his voice isn't up to it. The bloodlust leaves him like a breath of cool air, draining away Sax's strength with it. He's been cut, gashed one too many times. Sax can feel each and every bit leaking from his insides onto the metal floor around him. A tangy taste in his mouth. A blur at the edges of his eyes.

Bas appears in front of him, seeming to fall from above. She's jumped the center. Stayed well away from the Sevora. Smart.

"The Fassoth did its work well," Bas whispers, looking Sax over.

Nothing about her expression gives Sax hope.

"The mission, Bas," Sax replies. "Please."

Bas looks back at the Sevora, which seems to be ignoring them,

"I've never seen one like that before."

"You have to destroy it. It's the pilot, Bas. It's controlling this whole ship."

Knock out the Sevora, and perhaps the seed ship would fall into the gas giant's gravity well. A craft this large, no matter its armor, would hit that planet's strong atmosphere and tear to shreds. It's the one thing Sax could see working. Their one chance.

"Take the mask," Bas says and without waiting for Sax to reply, she presses her claws together.

The mask melts off of her and piles in front of Sax. He reaches for it, places his claws into the soft material. The mask flows up and around Sax, into his wounds, where it hardens. Acts as a salve, staunching the bleeding. Sax bears the pain, the agony of the mask sealing the wounds, with his eyes open and mouth taut. Bas has given him life, and he won't dishonor that gift by showing weakness.

"Thank you."

"It's not for you," Bas says, keeping her eyes on the parasite. "It's for me. When you're ready, I'll need your help."

"I'll be there." Though Sax can't guarantee that. His limbs are loose, weak, and the idea of getting up again sends a thin tremor through his nerves.

Bas rises to her full height and spreads her arms, claws glittering. That's when Sax notices the parasite hasn't been idle during their conversation. Orange and yellow strands have stretched from the stalks out towards them, angling towards the pools of Sax's blood on the floor. The strands fork, new offshoots poking out towards them. Growing fast.

Across the room, the Sevora envelopes the Fassoth's body with more.

Bas begins with the close tendrils, slicing through the ones on the ground with her lower arms. With every cut, the strands retract. Draw closer to the mushroom mass at the center.

"Caution," Sax hisses at his pair's back.

Bas' tail twitches an acknowledgment, and she goes slow, swiping as the strands come into range. Better to be deliberate than risk everything with a creature neither of them understand.

As Bas approaches, one of the red strings, dangling over the tubes, begins to shake, the bulge inside writhing harder. The end of the strand peels back, revealing a slug-like creature with tentacles of its own for a brief moment before it falls down the tubes. A new Sevora.

At the sight, Bas leaps forward, towards the central mass, and strikes the soft heads with her claws. They dig deep, scattering and tearing away milky-white glops of the Sevora. At first, it seems as though Bas will rip apart the entire creature in moments.

But the Sevora isn't done.

Strands shoot up from the floor, over from the Fassoth's body, from everywhere except the red ones hanging above the tubes. While Bas works her way into the creature, the Sevora fibers wrap around her arms, legs, and tail. At first, Bas rips them away, her claws carving a swath of the strands with a wide swing. The move, though, leave Bas' arms on her left side, and new strings rushed to fill the gap.

The Sevora pins Bas' limbs tight to her body. Bas bites at them, gnashing away fibers, until the strands fill her mouth, forcing it open. Sax knows he needs to move. Needs to help, but his arms and legs won't respond, and Bas is dying in front of him.

I carry the soup to Viera myself that evening. The Lunare lies in her cart, though her skin looks less like the color of death and more like warm milk.

"So did it work?" Viera asks when she sees me. "Did the Lunare run?"

"I thought they were your friends?" I set the clay bowl of soup in front of her.

"Friends change," Viera says. "Besides, none of them are as much fun as you."

"Fun?"

"Not every day you get to meet a high priestess. Not every day you get to run from juars in the Pits."

"Hopefully it's not every day you get so infected you nearly die." Viera shifts her shoulders, attempting to shrug. "It depends. You going to try to cauterize me again?"

I glance away, towards the fire. "Because of Ignos, we won't need to do that much longer. There are so many new things, Viera. So many discoveries waiting for us. We won't need the old ways."

Viera catches the change in tone. She takes a sip of the soup and her expression fades into a blank slate. Waiting for me.

"Things are going to get more dangerous from here on." It's soothing talking to Viera, someone who has no standing in Charre world, who's as out of place as I am. "Malo tells me the city's elders, in Damantum, they'll pick someone new. Another Emperor. One who won't much like me."

"Like you?"

I nod towards where the priests are eating around their own fire. They keep casting looks at me. Not favorable ones.

"They don't like my power. Now that the fight is over, they're realizing what it means to have someone like me around. Someone who has a god whispering in her mind. How can they compete with that? Who's going to listen to them now?"

"Who cares? Tell them to get real jobs."

I laugh, and it feels good to break free. It only lasts for a second, though, before I remember that Father is just like those priests, and he did everything for my village. "The Charre need their faith. If I tear the priests away, then who will listen to the people? Who will hear their prayers? Who will perform their ceremonies and tend to their sick? I can't be everywhere at once."

Viera doesn't have anything for that one. I keep going, then, to spare her the need to talk. Let her take another drink or two of the soup.

"So I have to work with them. I have to work with Jakkan when we return. He's going to be my only chance to rally everyone to my side."

"Tell me something," Viera says. "You're from some small village in the jungle. Your father is the head of a tribe. You have a family. Why bother with this? You already won. The Lunare won't come back for a long time. Why not just disappear?"

Because that is not who you are.

"Because Ignos will not let me." I hold my hands up to the coals. It's a chilly night, and the fire's warmth feels good. A little thing, but a normal thing. Good to have those every now and then.

"I don't think you get it. If they don't like you, then it won't matter which god is on your side. They'll find a way, and you'll die."

"I thought you'd protect me." I smile to take the edge off.

"Not going to be doing a lot of protecting like this." Malo interrupts by stomping near our little fire. A motion that kills any further conversation, and leaves both of us staring up at the warrior.

"Kaishi," Malo says, and he bows slightly. "I'm sorry to disturb you, we need your help. My warriors tell me one of the miracles isn't working. Perhaps Ignos will tell you how to fix it?"

I look at Viera. "You see, this is why I need the priests. Why I'll need so much help. Because I need to tend to my own miracles."

"Perhaps you need to make better ones then. Ones that don't break." I want to laugh with Viera again, but Malo's set face keeps me quiet.

The two of us walk through the camp, past fire after fire surrounded by warriors. Finally, we reach the outskirts, where a set of warriors are packing away the miracles. As we approach, they stop and look at me.

"Show her," Malo says. "You asked me to get her, now she's here. Show the priestess what you need repaired."

The lead warrior, a black bear skin over his head and shoulders, reaches into a crate and pulls out the shard. He holds up the handle.

"It no longer burns."

"Have you refilled the canister?" I ask.

At this, the warriors all look surprised. A simple problem I've already showed them how to resolve before. So why is this an issue now? It shouldn't be.

"Is that everything?" Malo's as exasperated as I am. "Even I could solve that for you."

"No, chieftain. It is not everything." The warrior drops the end of the shard, and then suddenly cracks it forward, towards me.

The others charge with him.

Sax can't see Bas anymore. The Sevora has covered her in its fibers. Sax can, though, still see movement in there. His pair struggling. He has to do something. Has to get up. Sax sweeps his tail, mostly unharmed, behind him and pushes. Rises onto his feet. His claws slip on his own blood and Sax falls onto his side. As he tips, Sax tries to catch himself, and his lower left arm brushes something on his side. A slight bulge in the mask. On the ground, Sax feels for it. Realizes what it is.

The Stim vial. Bas never used hers.

Sax jams his claw into the bag, feels the liquid coat it. Instead of gently withdrawing, Sax scoops his claw out and sticks it, drenched with the drug, into his mouth. A small amount increases concentration, removes pain. A large amount can kill, can send the user's muscles and hearts into such overdrive that they simply explode.

Now, though, Sax needs all the strength he can get.

The Stim burns through his body. Unlike the Oratus' natural bloodlust, the drug doesn't drive away Sax's senses. Rather, his blurred vision vanishes, and he stands again without effort. Whatever damage the motion causes to his muscles isn't going to hamper him.

Not now.

He turns towards the Sevora, towards Bas. Sax can charge, can try what Bas did, but that didn't work. Bas shredded the domed growths, but there are too many of those fibers. Sax needs another solution. He scans the room, finds nothing, and then looks up. Back towards their crashed evac mod, still cradled in broken beams and metal plating up in the ceiling.

A ceiling that meshes with the outer hull.

Beyond the evac mod, Sax can see what has closed the opening behind their crash: a pale gray plastic. Just like the assault shuttles, the stuff acts as a temporary seal against vacuum.

Temporary.

Sax leaps towards the wall, digs in his claws and scrambles up the side towards the top of the chamber. Climbs along the ceiling towards the evac mod. The craft still hangs there, hatch open, as if waiting to be used again. So Sax does use it; as a foothold to rise up into the broken bits of rubble and splintered wires. To the seal itself.

Thin and opaque, the seal feels like a rock when Sax presses his claw against it, but when he flexes the sharp points on his hand, they bit into the seal as they would a soft wood. He can break it. Expose the chamber to vacuum.

Down below, the Sevora is ignoring Sax. Its tendrils, the ones that aren't wrapping around Bas, are concerned with the Fassoth. Continuing to devour the thing's body. No doubt the parasite assumes Sax has nowhere to go. That he will, eventually, become the Sevora's next meal.

Sax latches onto the hull with his legs and his mid-claws, digging the points deep. He will have to hold against the pull, at least for a little while. The Sevora must die before Sax can let go.

With his fore claws, Sax begins to punch at the parts of the seal he can reach. Small holes, not quite through to space. When he'd peppered the surface, Sax lets his tail hang down, then swings it up hard. His tail smashes into the weakened seal and punches through. A third of the seal breaks away immediately, and in front of his eyes, Sax can see the spinning orange atmosphere of the gas giant.

Cold, hard space.

Vacuum feels like a thousand hands at Sax's back, pushing him towards the opening. His claws, though, hold. The rushing air blots out any other noises—a deafening roar as atmosphere flees the ship.

Sax keeps focus on the next step: the seal must remain open. Tiny robots, like spiders, crawl out of slits in the hull around Sax. They scamper to the hole and, from canisters attached to their backs, begin to spray sealant. Attempt to close the hole.

Sax isn't going to let them.

With his foreclaws and tail, Sax scatters the robots. Sweeps them away in bunches. The seed ship will send as many as it can to the breach until it seals, and there would be millions of the things on a ship this large, but Sax doesn't need to fight them forever.

Sax risks a glance at the Sevora and sees a mass of strands. All colors, all rising towards him, like a plant growing at an incredible rate. They rise around the evac mod, which shifts in its cradle as the vacuum pulls at it too. In a moment, the strands will reach Sax. In a moment, they will wrap themselves around him, and his desperate attempt might end. Even so, this is his only option, and Sax can't give up now.

So he keeps swiping at the robots, keeps the seal clear, and suddenly the strands are flowing past him. They attempt to bend; Sax sees them twist as the vacuum pulls them past, but the fibers aren't strong enough. One of the Sevora's mounds blows by, a larger chunk.

The rest of the Sevora follows—the vacuum pulling the entire creature up and out, sucking it through the open seal and into space.

Something's missing. Sax sees the strands go past, but no Bas.

Where is she?

Sax tears his eyes away from the disappearing parasite and looks down again. Bas is there, clinging to the evac mod, looking battered, but alive. She meets his look, and Sax sees her mouth open, but the vacuum roar blots out any sound. Sax waves with one claw, stops sweeping the robots away. In a few moments, they'll complete the seal again. Sax and Bas will be safe. He watches the little things get to work.

Until a massive, white shape flies up from the ground, bounces off of the evac mod into the broken seal and splits it all the way apart, sweeping the spider bots with it. Sax feels the thing strike his back, knocking his hold away, and then Sax is through, following the Fassoth's huge body into the open black of space.

There are moments when time seems to freeze. When everything slows and I find myself aware of all the things that escaped my notice seconds ago. I see the blank eyes of the four warriors arrayed against me, all of them dead set on mine. I see their mouths carving into growls and shouts, which drown in the noise of our army's victory celebration. I see their arms reaching towards me, or drawing their kukri.

Behind them, the desert stretches to the dark horizon, shaded gray from Nomis' glow mixing with roaring fires. The light from those same fires casts an angry orange upon my attackers, giving them the look of the devils my father used to harangue our village about. Demons and monsters that would take those who failed to pay the proper respects.

As they come for me now.

I fall away, stumbling back from the four attackers and, tripping on a rock, landing on my back. I don't stop, but press my hands against the dirt, pushing myself further. Anything to keep moving. In front of me, the warrior with the shard casts its black, glinting death.

Malo's kukri catches the strike as the shard whips forward,

knocking the attack aside. Malo follows his own block, setting his feet and swinging his other kukri towards the attacking warrior's chest. The hooked edge leaves a wide red gash as it cuts, and the shard-wielding warrior steps back, gets some space.

"What are you doing?" Malo shouts at the warriors, though he doesn't need to. The warriors themselves are answering his question on their own. They cry out infidel, blasphemer, assassin. Maker of foul things.

Dark names pour from their mouths as the four come for me. Malo's right kukri catches the shard as the warrior strikes, and the black-glass edges bite into the kukri's wooden haft. With a hard yank, the warrior pulls the kukri from Malo's hands. Two of the other warriors, their own kukri drawn, force Malo into a desperate defensive dance, with his single kukri working to deflect the strikes.

Leaving me with the last warrior, the brown fur skin nearly hiding his face as he moves toward me, kukri ready to strike.

"Stop!" I yell loud and clear. It's the only thing I can think to say.

The soft desert air carries my command above the singing and drinking, and my voice pierces the celebration.

My cry makes the attacker pause. He looks beyond me, doubtless at all the others now bearing witness to their deeds. His death for this is certain. His hesitation slides into desperation, and then resignation. He takes a stride, raises his weapon, and then grunts as a thrown kukri embeds itself in his side, and then he falls.

Malo.

He's to the left of me now, and he's thrown his only defense to grant me a little more time; a few more pushes of my feet against the ground, scrambling away from my enemy. I hear my friend scream, angry and pained, as the other warriors find their marks. Malo disappears to the dirt, the two warriors beating him to the ground.

You must move. To the crates. They are your only chance!

Ignos is right. I get to my feet, spy the other three crates nearby, and run towards them.

"High priestess, submit," the shard warrior says, advancing towards me as I close on the closest crate. As I grab the lip and push it open. "You've been speaking the words of devils. And now you have killed our leader. The holiest one himself. As Jakkan said it would to be, so it is. Answer for your crimes. Reclaim what honor you can."

Jakkan. Why would the high priest say the Emperor would die?

At the bottom of the crate, lying there on cloth woven for its bed, is the weapon Malo had used earlier that day. Fit to fire rounds, with a new case of them already loaded. I pull the weapon out, straining to lift it, and turn as the warrior raises the shard.

"Jakkan is spewing heresies and twisting your mind." I'm talking as I try to find the trigger, remember how this one works. "Think! Who but Ignos could create devices like the one you hold, like the one in my hands?"

The warrior's eyes slide to the weapon. Cold and gray in the dark, then he glances back up at me. "Such things are not meant for man."

His arm goes back, the shard flies high, and I find it, the smoothed metal that gives the slightest bit as my finger brushes it. The trigger. I press it in.

The gun kicks against my shoulder again and again, and I ignore the bruising pain. The gun's point bounces further up with every round, with every ear-splitting shot and echo and crack.

Red blossoms in front of me, and the warrior collapses into the dirt.

You can let go now. It's done.

Only then do I realize the gun itself has stopped firing. It's only clicking its empty magazine. I'd fired all twelve rounds. Most of them, going by the looks of my aim, arcing high into the sky.

The fighting is over.

The other two warriors are being pulled away by Charre, disarmed and captured. Other bear and lion soldiers close in front of me, barricading me with shields and spears in case these four are merely the first attempt.

My warriors—as I've already started thinking of them—escort me in a phalanx back to the priests, to Viera and her fire where they set up a ring around me, facing outwards and glaring at all comers. My priests offer tea, clamber to sacrifice the assassins with the dawn.

I nod. I agree.

I think only of Malo.

For a life lived in ships, Sax has never truly been in space. Never experienced the creeping chill of the great beyond, the black void. As he flies, he can only think about one thing:

Bas.

Sax has her mask. He'll survive in vacuum for a long time, with the armor protecting him from cold and recycling his air. Bas, though, will live only moments. Sax can't rotate his body, so he turns his head, tries to look towards the seed ship, already speeding into the distance, already falling into an orbital decay.

"This is Sax, hailing for rescue." Sax makes the call without thinking; standard procedure if they are knocked free from a ship.

The mask's communicators aren't long range, but Sax can see plenty of action around him. The battle continues. Someone will hear, will track the signal. Sax sees it then. A speck rising up from the seed ship. Heading his way, though Sax knows it won't reach him. The evac mod. Floating free from the larger craft. Its smaller size means its orbit will last longer, it might stay up. There's a chance, Sax knows, that Bas is in that mod.

He chooses to believe she is. The hope makes the long drift

through space easier, makes repeating his calls for rescue more urgent. It's about saving his pair now.

It seems like forever before a shuttle floats into view. Before another Oratus, this one tethered to the craft, grabs Sax from his endless orbit of the gas giant and pulls him inside. From there, a series of moments pass as Sax directs the crew to capture the evac mod before it descends too deep into the atmosphere. As the Flaum medical officer on the shuttle peels off Sax's mask and begins applying treatments. Numbing agents, stitches, and more. Sax barely pays attention. He stares at nothing, running replays of the last few moments on board the seed ship.

He'd seen her, Sax is sure. Clinging to the edge of the mod. Watching him. Waiting for the seal to close. Would she have had the time to get into the mod? Close the door before all of the atmosphere drained? If Bas hadn't given Sax her mask, she would have—no. That is foolishness.

The mask is the only thing that let Sax continue breathing that close to the vacuum, that allowed him the energy to finish the mission. Bas made the right choice.

The shuttle loads the evac mod through its tiny bay, meant more for landing craft than something like this. Sax pushes himself off of the medical table, ignoring the protests of the Flaum, and runs. The door to the bay slides open as Sax approaches, just as the pair of Flaum on the shuttle crack the hatch. The mod's entrance swings up, joints creaking, but Sax doesn't wait for it to finish moving before he dives inside.

He wraps his arms around his pair, careful to keep his claws from poking through her scales, and Sax carries Bas from the mod. Lifts her to the medical bay, and, when the Flaum waves at Sax to put Bas on the sole bed Sax himself has just left, Sax obeys.

Later, when Bas asks Sax what he'd been thinking at the moment, why he'd interrupted his own treatment to do what either of the other two Oratus were more than capable of doing, Sax replies that he wasn't thinking anything.

Instinct.

Instinct had saved his life, and now it had saved his pair's.

Low on oxygen, covered in strange pokes from the Sevora's tendrils, Bas goes directly from the shuttle's medical bay to the ship's hospital when they dock with Evva's commanding vessel. Sax, still weak himself, leans on Gar for support as he watches Bas, unconscious, receive precise attention from a swarm of robots. It isn't until one of the things, covered in arms and instruments, tells Sax that Bas will make an eventual recovery, that Sax feels the universe right its tilt. His ears stop ringing and, for what feels like the first time, Sax sucks a full breath through his vents.

Gar and Lan laugh, then. A happy hissing. Through the translucent wall behind them, a fiery bloom blossoms against the orange planet. The seed ship, derelict without its piloting parasite, crashes into the atmosphere.

Another mission accomplished.

I wake up surrounded by warriors and priests. Ignos rises as he has every day of my life to this point, but when he shines on me now, I'm told Ignos shines on an Empress. A woman who united the Charre and Solare. Who drove away their enemy. Who hears from Ignos himself.

Leaders from villages and tribes approach me in a train, each one bowing and offering allegiance. Malo is still clinging to life, so Viera stands near me, hand on her weapon. Surprise hits faces as people realize my closest guard is a Lunare, but right now I can't think of dealing with all of this alone. I barely know what to say. I thank them, and speak what Ignos tells me.

Ignos pushes, through me, for the tribes to pledge their loyalty. Not to the Charre, but to me. This too causes a stir, but when they remember the miracles, nobody questions it.

Part of me waits for Father. Did he join the Lunare as they swept through the jungle? Are the hunters of my village here in this gathering?

But they don't appear, and as the last leaders say their vows and begin taking their forces home, I'm left at the head of a Charre force that, too, needs to be moving. The sooner we get back to Damantum, the sooner Malo gets better care.

The sooner, Viera says, we can deal with Jakkan.

The two of us spend the march back together, with me in silent consultation with Ignos while Viera spins tale after tale. The woman seems to have a hatred of silence, and now that her illness has returned her voice, Viera never lets it rest. I don't mind the stories of the underground, the dark caves and high mountain cliffs.

When Ignos lets me listen, anyway.

The god is busy. He tells me plans, things I must do to keep his favor now that I have the power to make them happen. First come pools filled with strange mixtures of plants and minerals. Housed inside buildings, if possible. Then will come forges and factories. Massive structures that will transform the Charre into a state unrecognizable. Ignos's vision is sprawling, but it is a vision.

I made my way here, to the top of a throne I never wanted, and guaranteed the safety of the Solare tribes. My plan is complete. Ignos tells me what comes next, and I'm grateful for it. After two days—the wounded make our return a slow one—the walls of Damantum appear. The first time I saw those walls, they struck me breathless. Now, it's unease. A nausea that I recognize from before the sacrifice, from when I first spoke as a priestess to my village.

Actions are about to be taken that I cannot reverse.

At midday we reach Damantum's towering gates. They're closed, and Jakkan, with a cluster of priests and curious citizens, stands on top, staring down at me.

Break him, Kaishi. You cannot allow threats to your power to stand. He tried to kill you. Us.

"Hold here," I announce. I don't want my first act as Empress to be an attack on my own city.

I walk out in front of my force, and only Viera follows me. The two of us are alone on the sallow grass, an easy target for an assassin, though I feel Jakkan would have to be truly brazen to attack in front of everyone.

"Jakkan," I shout. "Tell me why the gates of my city are closed to me?"

"The holy city does not open to heretics," Jakkan replies. "You know I cannot let you return, Kaishi. You know that the source of all your strength is a dark one. Without the threat posed by your supposed gifts, the Lunare would not have killed our Emperor. They would have been our allies. Instead, you drive us to war and corrupt the city and its people in your quest to rule."

"I do not try to rule," I answer.

Jakkan's words catch me off guard. It's a strange argument to make. Why would I have gone out to fight the Lunare, if it was my intent to take over? As I look at the people standing on the wall, and glance back at my own force, I realize Jakkan isn't talking to me.

Before I come up with an answer, the high priest repeats his accusations, going into even more florid detail about the many atrocities I will commit to secure my place at the head of the city. As he speaks, I see the conflicted stares of my own army, of the crowds on the walls.

Jakkan is trying to do more than prevent my entry.

He is converting my empire.

You inspired a village, a city, and an army, Kaishi. Do not let this fool stand in your way.

Ignos is right.

"Then tell me this, Jakkan," I interrupt. "You say the miracles, brought to us by Ignos through me, are the work of evil, yet they cast the Lunare from our lands. They avenged the Emperor. They save the lives of our people each and every day. How can that be evil?"

Jakkan opens his mouth to rebut me, but I keep talking. I understand the high priest's trick now. Establish momentum, draw the audience in, and let no one divert me from my course.

"Why did the Emperor, the holiest of holies, choose to bring me with him instead of you?" I scan the faces of the crowd as I shout, meet as many eyes as I can find. "Perhaps it was because you were disloyal. Because he did not trust you heard the true words of Ignos. You, who sent assassins to kill me."

By Jakkan's face, I know I am correct.

"Lies. Lies and slander cast upon me by this newcomer. She isn't even a Charre herself. She is a Solare! Not one of us!" Jakkan sweeps his arms high, beseeching the crowd. "Stand with me and cast out this usurper, this witch, who threatens to—"

A familiar crack echoes across the plain. The shot strikes Jakkan in the shoulder and the high priest lurches back from the parapet and falls out of sight.

Viera, her pistol drawn, shrugs at me. "Thought he was calling you an awful lot of names. Didn't find that to my liking."

Being placed on medical hold is, to Sax, the worst form of punishment. He'd let himself get hurt—mauled by a Fassoth, really—and, as a result, is quartered in the medical wing of Evva's ship. Healing isn't even the priority —Sax endures pokes and prods, injections and examinations to see whether exposure to a mature Sevora could result in something strange.

Which is why Sax isn't surprised when the door to his quarantine room opens without any warning. Consisting of a bed, table, and an Oratus-fitted chair, Sax watches the feed of the battle—now winding down, with ships either retreating or cleaning up scrap—playing on the quarter of one wall serving as a screen.

"Sax, you've been cleared," Evva, her crimson scales bright in the light, explains as she walks into the room. It's tight with both of them in here, and they swish their tails around until they find a clear landing space. "Bas, however, is still recovering, but we can't wait for her before moving. Thanks to the defector, we know now that this wasn't what we hoped for. There are still more Sevora ships out there, Sax, and now we know where they are."

"Defector?"

"The infected Oratus, Avan," Sax catches Evva's glance behind them before she says his name.

Checking for eavesdroppers.

"There are cameras in here, commander," Sax says. "But nobody's going to check them if nothing irregular happens."

Evva stays taut, her claws clenching, but she continues, "He's been providing very interesting information that I'm working to verify. The implications, Sax, could be enormous, and I tell you this for one reason: I trust you, and few others."

"He wanted to save the Sevora," Sax replies. "What is he telling you?"

"That there may yet be a reason to stay our hand," Evva hisses. "Of course, he could be wrong, and if he is, I shall enjoy handling the execution personally."

"You're not going to tell me, are you?"

"Too many ears, Sax. But I didn't come here to talk about Avan. I have more mundane orders for you. We've learned about a seed that made landfall on a planet known to have intelligent, if pre-awakened, life. We rather the Sevora didn't corrupt the world entirely."

Sax sits back on the bed. Looks at his claws. "I'm not a cleaner. There are many others, less experienced, that could do this. Why me?"

Evva moves closer, sets a clawed hand on Sax's shoulder, leans in and whispers "Because I need you alive, Sax, for what might come next. Keeping you from the front is the easiest way to do that, and this assignment serves as a viable excuse."

Evva straightens and announces, loudly, "I know it isn't the assignment you wanted, but the fleet is moving quickly and we don't have time to wait for your recovery. This mission will be an easy way to ease you back into active duty. Bas too."

Sax, left with few options, stands as Evva moves to leave the room.

"I will complete the mission to the best of my abilities, commander."

"As ever, Sax. I honor your life." Evva bows as she says the formal words.

"It is my honor to give it." Sax bows in kind, and then Evva is gone.

Do I know what it means to be an Empress? To lead the Charre, not my own people, as I'm barely seventeen summers?

No.

But I have a god speaking through me. I have a bracelet full of miracles. And as I step outside the Vaos' chambers, an adoring crowd chants my name. Promises my every command will be carried out. In the days after my return, I presented small miracles furnished by the Cache to Damantum's elders.

One by one, I swayed their opinions with medicinal ointments, plans for new, personal miracles, and, in some cases, with gold and artifacts that Jakkan, who had met his fate under the black-glass knife, had left behind. When the time came to choose a new leader for Damantum, no one else even bothered to submit their name.

On my left stands my personal guard, a Lunare named Viera. Her old, ruined clothes replaced by the finest Charre cape and cloth. Green, like my own. On my right stands the leader of my armies, though Malo is kept upright, for now, by a pair of lion warriors.

Together we stare over my city, over the walls to the vast fields where the changes are already starting. Black smoke rises, thunderous fires burn deep; new miracles being born.

All ours, Kaishi. All ours.

Read on for an excerpt from MIND'S EYE, *the* SKYWARD SAGA *Book Two— available FREE by signing up for my new release news-letter through the* QR *Code below:*

AN EXCERPT FROM
MIND'S EYE
THE SKYWARD SAGA BOOK TWO

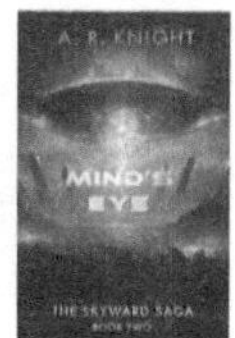

They land the shuttle in the dark of night over the crater where the seed crashed. Bas found the site from orbit—a rippling, fresh pit where the devastation from the strike is still visible beneath new growth.

It's clear to Sax, as soon as the boarding ramp goes down, that the seed hit some time ago. It's already overgrown with small plants and ferns. Vines stretch around the mottled gray outside of the craft. A small nest of furry creature scatters as Sax claws his way to the ship.

Insects cluster around him, drawn by the shuttle's low blue lights, which provide visibility without being overly conspicuous. Sax brushes away the foliage. Confirms that the seed opened. Confirms that it's empty of the life-sustaining nutrients.

"It's been triggered," Sax says. "The Sevora is gone."

Bas, waiting at the top of the pit, doesn't seem surprised. "We detected plenty of evidence of life on the way here. Likely, someone stumbled upon it."

"It's been here a while, if the growth here is consistent with other worlds," Sax replies. "Enough time for the Sevora to immerse itself."

The subtext: the two Oratus have to be ready for resistance.

They return to the shuttle, gear up with a pair of miners—heat-blasting rifles—apiece, and Sax grabs his black bars, the ones that, if needed, can cut through anything this planet would care to throw at them.

From there the Oratus head into the jungle. There's no trail, and the thick, snarled plants mean it's been some time since any thing has made its way to the crash site. So, instead, Sax listens. The sounds of the jungle crash over him in waves. The hoots of mysterious creatures, sharp, chirping calls of others, the whistling of wind shooting between tree trunks, making branches and leaves clatter their way from canopy to ground. It's a lovely chorus, even if it doesn't help Sax determine where to go.

But there's something else beneath the sounds—a low, consistent pulse that shakes his legs.

Music.

Bas hears it too, and they both glance at each other, their eyes acknowledging their shared intuition, then head towards the sound. It's slow going – the growth is thick, and the two Oratus commit to staying quiet. It's unclear what kind of resistance they might face, what level of technology. Best to surprise a potential enemy than the other way around.

As they close, the music grows louder, and now there's singing to go with it. Words Sax is surprised to find he recognizes. A cheerful song, of harvests and thanks. Of gifts.

"Sevora gifts," Bas hisses.

Sax agrees. They keep moving and Sax falls into the mystery of the hunt. The strange sweet zone where time dilates and all of his instincts come into focus. Where the slightest whisper of wings feels like the loudest thunderclap.

Which is when he notices they are being tracked.

Sax looks to his left and sees a strange species standing there. Counts two arms, two legs and what appears to be a head growing out of a sizable torso. Smaller than Sax himself. Though, going by the steady eyes staring back at him, this species is not afraid of the Oratus.

The creature holds a short spear, and it angles the weapon towards Sax. Shoves the spear, point first, towards the Oratus. Not close enough to hurt, and Sax recognizes the warning. Step closer, the creature is saying, and that point will make its way into Sax's chest.

Sax's mask would likely turn the spear, and Sax would, doubtless, be able to tear the creature apart. But if Sax can see one, there might be others. Starting an uncertain fight in the dark, risking their lives and health, would be a poor plan.

Though he wouldn't mind if the creature started one.

"What are you?" the creature says. Sax is momentarily stunned to hear the galactic common tongue spoken on this strange world.

It signals Sevora, and Sax tenses.

"Stop," Bas says as she senses Sax's plan. "No Sevora would ask what we were. It would know, it would react."

She's right. Sax straightens, and notices the creature has fallen into its own battle stance. One hand up to its lips, forming a circular gesture, and the other holding the spear, point toward Sax, low and ready to stab.

"We are visitors," Bas hisses. "Newcomers to your land. Who are you?"

"We? We are the Solare. This is our jungle. Our village. Why have you come?"

Neither Sax nor the warrior relax. Both ready to jump at each other's throats. Bas, though, let's her tail touch Sax's own. Calm down, the gesture says, don't make enemies we don't need.

"We are called Oratus," Bas answers. "We come from far away. Beyond the sky. We are searching for another who came from the stars. Who promises wonders."

Bas' answer works. The creature steps forward, but as it does so, it raises the short spear's point up. "I'm sorry, but you are too late. Who you were looking for left long ago."

Sax straightens up as well. "The one we're looking for?"

The creature seems to remember something. Its face flicks

towards the village. Towards the music and sound. "I'll take you. There are others here who would be better at explaining than I."

"We would be grateful," Bas says.

They follow the creature through the last bit of jungle. Along the way, they ask and the creature tells them what they are. Humans. Their tribe and people named Solare. Men and women, daughters and sons. The man speaks so freely and Sax doesn't understand why until their escort calls them gods.

Ah.

Sax does nothing to dispel the thought.

They head into a wide clearing from which rise a number of crude stone buildings and one strange, tall mass of wood, moss and rock. In front of it appears the rest of the tribe. The whole group of them dancing and chanting around pleasing pits of fire. Roasting meats, fruits and burning incense fill the six breathing vents stitching Sax's chest with smells.

At least for a moment, because all of it stops as soon as Sax and Bas come into the firelight. As soon as everyone stares at them. In the quiet, there in a clearing, Sax picks up rustling from around them. He looks, and at the borders of the village stand other humans, holding bows with arrows aimed at the two Oratus.

They've walked into a trap.

Continue Kaishi and Sax's adventures with MIND'S EYE, free with newsletter sign-up or for purchase at your favorite retailer:

ACKNOWLEDGMENTS

This novel is the product of my family and friends refusing to let a dream die. My wife Nicole, for letting me write in the early mornings and making sure I didn't starve. My brothers and parents for their continual comments, support, and enthusiasm.

And, of course, you, the reader, for giving me a reason to write.

A.R. Knight spins stories in a frosty house in Madison, WI, primarily owned by a pair of cats. After getting sucked into the working grind in the economic crash of the 2008, he found himself spending boring meetings soaring through space and going on grand adventures.

Eventually, spending time with podcasting, screenplays, short stories and other novels, he found a story he could fall into and a cast of characters both entertaining and full of heart.

Thanks, as always, for reading!

For more information:
www.adamrknight.com

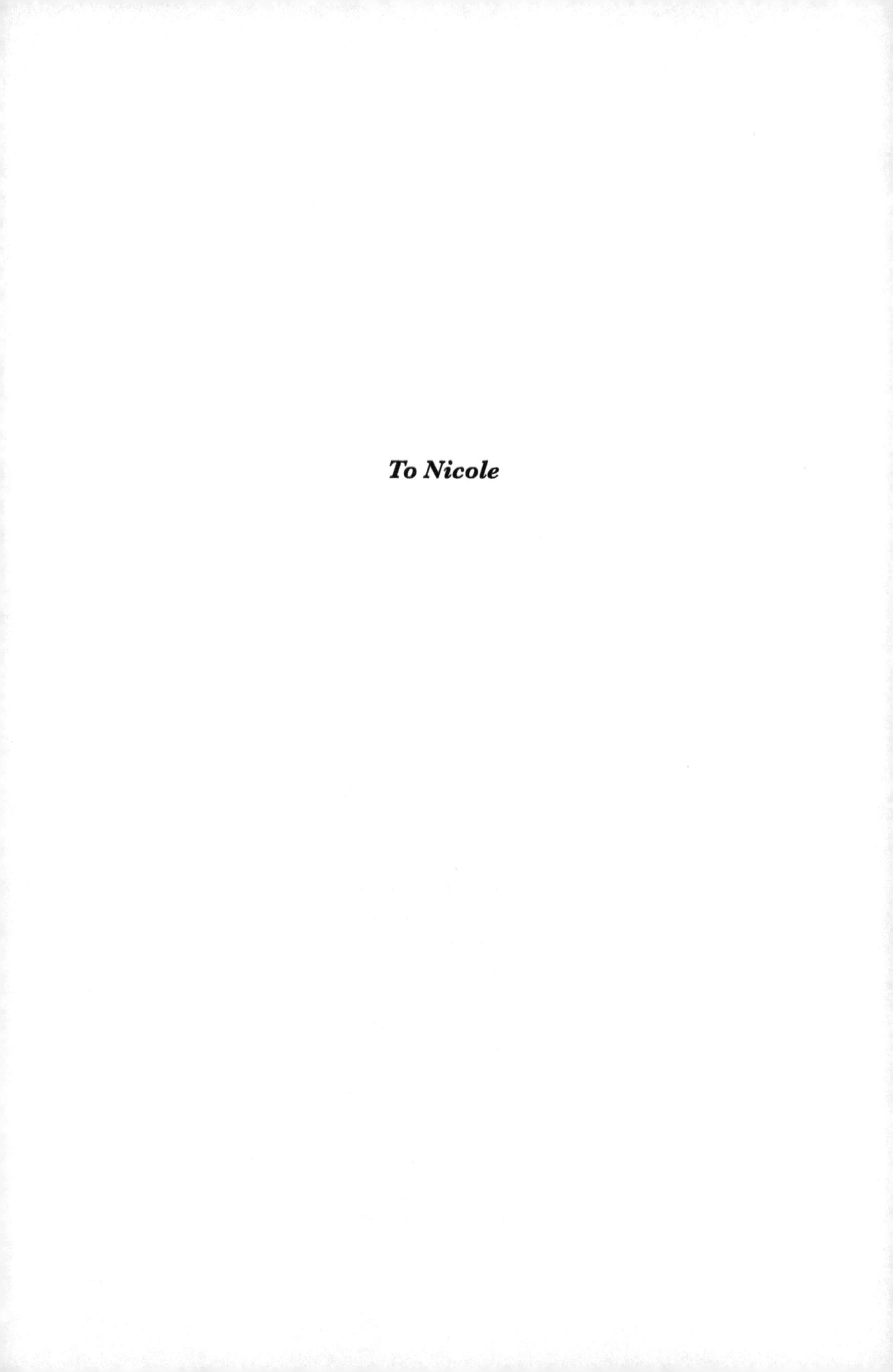

To Nicole